Say You Love Me

Copyright © 2018 by Mirror Press, LLC
Print edition
All rights reserved

No part of this book may be reproduced in any form whatsoever without prior written permission of the publisher, except in the case of brief passages embodied in critical reviews and articles. This is a work of fiction. The characters, names, incidents, places, and dialogue are products of the author's imagination and are not to be construed as real.

Interior design by Cora Johnson

Edited by Cassidy Wadsworth Skousen and Lisa Shepherd

Cover design by Rachael Anderson

Cover image credit: Deposit Photos #31588957

Published by Mirror Press, LLC

ISBN-13: 978-1-947152-33-5

Say You Love Me

A PINE VALLEY NOVEL

Heather B. Moore

Mirror Press

PINE VALLEY SERIES

Worth the Risk
Where I Belong
Say You Love Me

Say You Love Me

Clara Benson is not looking for a relationship, especially not after losing her teaching position, followed by a disastrous breakup with her fiancé, and the sudden death of the grandma who raised her. In fact, Clara picks up and moves to escape her mess of memories. She hopes Pine Valley will be the perfect place to heal from heartache.

When she meets her boss's lawyer, Dawson Harris, Clara can't deny her attraction. Yet she's determined to choose herself, and her healing, over a guy who might be charming, attractive, and oh, so appealing. Easy, right? But when Dawson becomes the one person who can straighten out her mess, she realizes that finding herself doesn't have to mean losing Dawson.

One

"Now . . . let's move into downward dog," the yoga instructor said, and Clara Benson stretched into position.

Clara had been taking the yoga class at the Pine Valley Recreation Center for three months now, yet she was not any more flexible than she had been when she'd started. But she could feel her core strength returning, and over all, her stress was becoming manageable. The dim lighting of the yoga room, the soft music, and the calm voice of the instructor probably had a lot to do with the stress relief as well. Five minutes into the class, and Clara could feel the weight on her shoulders slide off her like a warm shower. She would never admit to her boss, Jeff Finch, how hard it had been running the office mostly on her own while he dealt with a lawsuit and some personal problems.

Jeff Finch was an up-and-coming real estate agent in Pine Valley, and Clara was more than grateful he'd hired her six months ago even though her only qualification was being willing to try something new.

Pine Valley had been a new start for Clara. Seven months ago, her life had been in shambles. A failed engagement, her grandma's death, and losing her job teaching kindergarten at a charter school because the school had been under investigation—and all of it happening in the same week. After her grandmother's funeral, Clara had packed her things, turned the house over to a local realtor, and spoken the words into her phone: "I need to get away."

Pine Valley had popped up as a suggestion.

Clara had opened it in her Maps app and started driving. After three hours of driving the California freeways, she had turned into the community of Pine Valley. Two days later, she'd been hired by Jeff Finch, town realtor.

Even though Clara missed a lot of things about home, she knew she could never return. The memories of the grandma who raised her were too painful, not to mention the colossal breakup with Max. And although Clara was a certified elementary school teacher, she wasn't up to going back to the class-room and putting a smile on her face every day in front of young children. They saw through fake instantly.

But sitting behind a desk and talking on the phone with realtor clients? Clara could fake a cheerful tone all day.

Here, in the yoga room, she didn't have to put on a happy face in the dim room. She could close her eyes, listen to her body, focus on breathing, and empty her mind of her past.

Here . . . she could recreate a new Clara. A Clara who could rebuild her life and start over.

The soft click of the door was audible over the low music, but Clara didn't open her eyes. Someone had come late to class. Unusual, because Leslie, their instructor, was adamant that no one come in late. If you were late, you had to wait until the next session since Leslie didn't want the ambiance disturbed.

Although Clara's eyes were closed, she felt the presence of whomever had entered, felt the hesitation and possible confusion. The woman must be looking for a spot. There was room right behind Clara, but if the woman was new, it would be harder to follow Leslie's lead from the back of the room.

And then Clara heard the other women around her shifting their mats. She opened her eyes to see that the woman to her right had broken her pose to move her mat closer to Clara to make room for the new arrival.

Instantly Clara was annoyed. Although she closed her eyes during most of her poses, she didn't want to be too close to anyone else. She didn't want to hear someone else breathing or moving. It cut into her concentration.

Then, Clara caught sight of the new arrival—a man—who was setting a mat on the floor kitty corner to her.

Even in the dim light, she could see that the man looked like he worked out plenty. He wore gym shorts, and his sculpted form showed through his fitted T-shirt.

He moved easily into the next yoga position Leslie called out. In fact, he was absolutely lithe, which only made Clara self-conscious about her own awkwardness.

Two men were regulars in the class that was otherwise made up of women. But their average builds and average looks had never drawn the attention this newcomer did. All of the women kept glancing over at him, trying to be discreet in their curiosity. The new arrival had caught everyone's attention.

Including Clara's.

She hid a sigh of frustration. The last thing she needed in her yoga class—her one place of solace—was someone distracting her.

If Leslie had been bothered by the interruption, she hadn't shown it. In fact, now that Clara focused on the instructor, it seemed that Leslie was smiling just a little.

And, there it was.

Leslie was looking at the new arrival with a half-smile on her face. She knew him! Maybe he was her boyfriend?

That would explain it, although Clara hated that Leslie would bend her rules for even a boyfriend. And having him in this class might mean that Leslie, too, would now be distracted . . . not to mention the other women, who were suddenly doing deeper stretches and longer poses than Clara had ever seen them do before. And she should know, since she always set up at the back of the room. She didn't like the feeling of someone observing her poses. It helped with her concentration to think that no one watched her movements.

Clara knew she needed to clear her mind, to not worry about who may or may not be in the class, to just focus on her workout. If she didn't, the tension would return, and she'd have another lousy night again. Insomnia had been her close friend the last few weeks. Ever since February 1, the date of her grandma's birthday. The woman would have been seventy-four. Young, really. But the stroke had paralyzed her so severely that a second stroke a couple days later had been a blessing.

As much as Clara hated to think her grandma's death had been a blessing, she knew the spunky Phoebe Benson would have never been happy living as a paralytic.

The music shifted, and Leslie called out the next position, which meant that now Clara needed to turn in the direction of the new class member. She turned before he did and was surprised when she caught him looking at her.

She quickly looked away, but he didn't. Out of her peripheral vision, she felt him watching her, and Clara began to heat up. She never really perspired in yoga class. Tonight would be an exception.

She suddenly decided she would go to the later session on Fridays. She never had any plans anyway, and McKenna taught the later class. Clara wouldn't have to deal with this new man in class whom Leslie seemed to know.

Finally he looked away, which only meant Clara caught herself stealing glances in his direction. How was he so good at yoga? She'd never seen him in class before, and she'd come religiously for three months, four to five sessions a week.

Clara forced herself to not look in the man's direction again and kept her eyes closed as much as possible. But as fate would have it, his close proximity meant she was pretty much aware of all of his movements anyway.

"And that's it for today," Leslie said in a soft, low voice. "The lights will stay dimmed for another few minutes so you slowly release from your meditation. See you next time, everyone."

Clara opened her eyes as Leslie stood and took off her headset. The instructor then walked through the maze of mats toward the man next to Clara.

Leslie leaned down and talked to the man for a minute in hushed tones. Whatever was being said, it was flirty. Leslie was positively beaming—even in the dimness of the room, that was clear.

The man's hushed tones were deep and resonated through Clara, even though she couldn't distinguish what he was saying. Then Leslie straightened and went back to the front of the room. She said goodbye to the class members as they passed her to exit.

Clara decided she'd be the last one to leave the room. It would give her a few minutes by herself to re-center her thoughts. The next class would be in thirty minutes, and maybe she'd even stay for it. The double session might be what she needed tonight—she should sleep pretty well if she was completely exhausted.

But no, apparently super-yoga-man was staying as well. Leslie was talking to one of the final women in the room when Clara determined to leave after all. There was no way she was staying if her neighbor was staying as well. She rose to her feet and bent to roll up her mat, pointedly not looking over at the newcomer.

"Clara?"

She froze. Then, slowly, she raised her gaze to see the man looking right at her. Even though it was dim, she'd certainly recognize him if they knew each other. Which they didn't.

"Don't you work for Jeff Finch?"

Clara straightened, still studying the man's features. Surely she'd remember a man who looked like he could be a model and a professional athlete all in the same package.

He moved to his feet in one fluid motion. When he stood, he was well over a foot taller than Clara, although her 5'1" frame had never given her much of a height advantage over anyone.

Just then Leslie brightened the lights, throwing the room into stark visibility, and Clara got a good look at the man. His dark-brown eyes were intense, to say the least, and his hair was a dark blond—cut short, but just long enough to give him a bit of a playboy look.

"Dawson Harris," he said, extending his hand.

Clara's mouth opened; then she closed it. *Dawson Harris.* Jeff's lawyer? They'd talked on the phone a few times, and she'd always enjoyed their short conversations. If she'd known he looked like *this*, she might have been more reserved. He could easily be a poster boy for a country club, and perhaps he did spend a lot of time there with clients. His chiseled looks probably got him plenty of attention from women. Well, he knew her as bubbly, outgoing Clara, so that's who she'd be.

"Oh, hi, Mr. Harris," Clara said, putting on a broad smile, even though she was wearing workout clothes and her dark red hair was in a sweaty ponytail. Yet, now that the lights were on, she noticed his shirt had sweat stains too—maybe he'd been lifting weights or something before class. "Small world. I didn't know you were in this class."

"Small world, indeed," he said, his eyes crinkling at the corners with his smile. "I thought it was you—but since I've only seen your picture on the real estate website, I wasn't completely sure."

Clara laughed. Which mortified her, because it bordered on a giggle. "It's me, in person." She tucked her rolled mat under her arm. The sooner she got out of here the better, because Dawson Harris was making no secret of studying her—when his girlfriend was on the other side of the room.

"This class was a lot harder than I thought it would be," Dawson continued.

Clara almost laughed again and was about to say something about how he made it look easy—but would that be too flirty? "I thought yoga would be easy, too, before I tried it."

Dawson nodded and set his hands on his hips.

Clara refused to notice the definition of his arms. He was attractive, so what? A lot of men were. She didn't need to ogle her boss's lawyer. "Well, Leslie's a great teacher," she said, trying to think of an exit plan.

"Yeah, I guess so." He gave a half shrug. "I have nothing else to compare it to. This is my first class."

"Dawson!" Leslie called out, waving him over.

Time for Clara to make herself scarce.

Two

Dawson drew away from Leslie's rather tight grip. He had no problem hugging his condo neighbor, especially since she'd been begging him to come to her class for months and he'd finally made it. But he was probably not smelling too great, since he'd run several miles before showing up to the yoga class.

"I'm so glad you came," Leslie gushed, her dark ponytail bouncing as she talked. "I thought you said you were working late tonight."

"My client rescheduled," Dawson said. He'd been on his way to his meeting when Leslie had waved him down in the condo parking lot. Dawson did have a late meeting, but when it was cancelled, he made the detour to the gym. He preferred running outside, but he'd put off Leslie long enough. And he figured if he went to one of her classes, she'd stop being so persistent. Even though Leslie was about five years older than Dawson, who was thirty, she seemed to have the energy of a twenty-year-old.

"Great," she said. "I'm so glad you could make it. Can you come to my Saturday class too? I mean, you really need to come a few times to know if yoga works for you. I teach Tuesday and Friday nights, and Saturday mornings."

Dawson knew. Leslie recited her teaching schedule every time they ran into each other. He wondered if there was anything she talked about that wasn't yoga-related. Leslie was a pretty woman, enthusiastic, but he hadn't seen much depth so far. This alone had made him wary—that and the fact it seemed most people in his condo complex were divorced men and women, with a lot of on-again, off-again relation-ships in the mix.

Dawson had found out the hard way at a neighborhood barbeque a couple of weeks after he'd moved in. He was hit on by no fewer than five women throughout the night. And two of them made it clear they only wanted a hookup—no commitment.

Fresh from his own divorce less than a year ago, Dawson wanted to stay clear of even casual dating. He accepted most of the blame for his marriage falling apart. And since the separation, he had become even more of a workaholic. He'd finally decided it was time for some balance and promised himself he'd go running several times a week. Rain, snow, or sun.

The exercise had helped. Not only had it reduced stress and helped him sleep better, but his mind seemed sharper, and he was more patient with his mom. He wasn't sure if that was a direct result of increased serotonin in his brain, but he'd finally gone on two dates his mom had set up. Three months ago, but still. And now she was bugging him again, reminding him that there was no reason he couldn't have a healthy marriage with a kid on the way.

"Do you want to get something at the juice bar with me?" Leslie asked, her gaze hopeful.

Dawson was tempted to say yes, if only to not hurt her feelings, but that spark of hope in her eyes might only lead to more expectations on Leslie's part. And Dawson already knew that his friendship with Leslie would never move up a notch.

"I've still got a ton of paperwork to get through before tomorrow morning," Dawson said, glancing past Leslie.

It appeared that Clara had already left. A stab of disappointment shot through Dawson. Clara had been friendly and efficient on the phone every time they'd talked, and more than once Dawson had teased her by saying he should hire her as his own assistant. Clara had always laughed it off but continued to be sweet and friendly. So tonight, after introducing himself, he was surprised that she had acted standoffish. He hadn't expected the woman on the phone to act less friendly in person.

He already knew she was a striking redhead from the picture on the realtor website, and seeing her in person, even in a workout setting, had only made him more curious about her. Her eyes were a deep blue that reminded him of a dark turquoise, and she was more petite than he expected, maybe just over five feet tall. Her smile was quick, almost business like, but he liked the fact that she didn't seem to be wearing any makeup. Her natural beauty was just as attractive as her full makeup in the website picture. He'd have to ask Jeff if she had a boyfriend. Dawson could hear Jeff's groan now. Jeff always complained that Dawson could pick up a woman with the snap of his fingers.

The problem was, Dawson wasn't interested in a woman who'd jump to his every request. Maybe it was because Clara deflected his teasing that he was curious about her. Curiosity wasn't a bad thing, was it?

"Are you sure?" Leslie placed a hand on his arm. "The green razzleberry is perfect after a workout. And my next class doesn't start for thirty minutes."

Dawson didn't need to rethink his decision. If he hurried, maybe he'd catch Clara still in the parking lot. "Thanks for the offer," he told Leslie. "But I've got a pretty busy night ahead of me. I'll see you around the complex."

"Oh, okay," Leslie said, giving him what he could only term puppy-dog eyes. Then she leaned forward and hugged him again.

This second hug wasn't entirely necessary, but Dawson didn't want to be rude. Overall, he hadn't minded the yoga, especially right after running. It had helped with stretching that he usually neglected.

He strode out of the workout room, then down the hall and through the lobby. By the time he reached the parking lot, he knew he'd already missed Clara. He didn't think any of the cars remaining were hers. It had been worth a try, although he wasn't entirely sure why he'd felt so determined to catch up with her.

Dawson climbed into his new truck—well, new since the divorce. It was something he had bought just for himself. Romy hated trucks, so he'd sold his old one before they married. But now . . . Romy was no longer in his life, and he could buy a truck if he wanted to. Besides, it reminded him of his childhood and how his grandpa would pick him up in his old truck on Saturdays for their fishing trips.

Before Dawson started driving, he checked his list of incoming emails. No texts. One voicemail from his mom.

He cringed as he played the message back.

"Dawson, dear. I need you to call me right away. Dad and

I have four tickets to the spring symphony, so we were thinking you could come with a date. Madge Smith told me Paula is in town for the week—I guess her kids are out of school for fall break. I ran over there today and met Paula's kids. They're adorable. Although I never thought I'd tell my son to date a divorced woman with kids, you know that the divorce wasn't Paula's fault. And her kids are perfectly well-behaved." His mother released a happy sigh.

It made Dawson feel slightly ill. Not that he was opposed to having his own kids, or even possibly dating a woman who had a kid. But he was absolutely opposed to Paula Smith, or whatever her last name was now. They'd dated his senior year in high school, and when he'd found out she was dating two other guys at the same time, he'd vowed to steer clear of her.

His mother was still leaving her very lengthy message when the voicemail cut off. Dawson chuckled to himself. Only his mother could leave such long messages.

He'd call her after he got something to eat. Even though he'd turned down Leslie's invitation, he was hungry. And since he was too hungry to spend extra time cooking, it looked like he was getting a chicken sandwich at a drive-thru.

He connected his Bluetooth, then called Jeff Finch as he drove. Jeff was as much of a workaholic as Dawson, so he doubted the man would be out and about. Besides, Jeff always answered calls from his lawyer.

"Bad news?" Jeff said, picking up on the second ring.

"What?" Dawson was momentarily confused. "Oh. No. We won't hear back from Kyle's lawyer for another few weeks, but like I said, I don't think the lawyer's going to work pro bono." Jeff Finch had recently won a lawsuit against his business partner, Kyle, who also happened to be his cousin. Kyle had embezzled hundreds of thousands of dollars from Jeff's realtor business. And Kyle had threatened to countersue.

The problem was that Kyle was broke, and any decent lawyer could see that Jeff's case was solid.

"Oh, okay," Jeff said. "I was just worried when I saw your number on my phone on a Friday night."

"Yeah, well, I'm not calling about work stuff," Dawson said. He was suddenly wondering if he'd made a mistake and acted too hastily. "I was just in a yoga class at the rec center."

Jeff laughed. "Yoga? You? That would be entertaining to see."

"Funny," Dawson deadpanned. "My neighbor was teaching the class. She's been begging me to come for months."

"*She*? Do I sense an interest?"

"Leslie? Not unless you like a woman who has more energy than a Chihuahua."

Jeff laughed again, then said, "Did you change your mind about golfing tomorrow? Cameron's confirmed."

"Uh, no. I still can't come." Dawson cleared his throat. "I saw your secretary tonight at the yoga class. You know, Clara."

"Don't call her a secretary," Jeff said with a scoff. "She'll bite your head off. She's an office manager, or you might be able to get away with calling her an executive assistant."

"Duly noted." Dawson swallowed. He might get a lot of crap when he asked his next question. "Is she, uh, in a relationship?"

Dawson turned down the volume of his Bluetooth while Jeff laughed.

When Jeff regained control of his delight, he said, "*Clara*? I dare you to ask her out, but don't come crying to me with your hurt ego after."

"Why? What's up with her?" Dawson said. "Is she into other women, or something?"

"Is that the only reason you can fathom that a single woman would turn you down?"

"No," Dawson was quick to say, but he hadn't missed the laughter still in Jeff's voice. "Look, tonight was the first time I met her in person. We seem to get along great over the phone, but I never really . . . Well, let's just say I wasn't all that curious until I met her in person."

Jeff was quiet for so long that Dawson wondered if the call had been dropped.

"Hello?" he said as he pulled into the parking lot of a fast food restaurant. He got into line behind a few other cars.

"Okay, I'll give you the scoop, but just because I don't really see the two of you together anyway," Jeff said. "I mean, you're a great guy, Dawson, and you're very gregarious—if you know what I mean—and it's perfect for the courtroom. But Clara is . . . she actually keeps to herself a lot and is a private person. She's great with clients though. On the phone she's perfectly charming."

Dread pooled in Dawson's stomach. Maybe the good feelings he had toward Clara were only because he was being sweet-talked as well.

"But there's another side to her," Jeff continued. "One I haven't figured out yet. I think she's battling some heavy stuff. Whenever I ask about her past, she shuts right up. I finally put a couple of things together and realized that she moved to Pine Valley on a fluke. Like packed and moved in one night. Stayed at a hotel until I hired her, and then she found an apartment to rent."

"Interesting," Dawson said. "Do you think she's running from someone? Maybe her name's not really Clara?"

"Nothing like that," Jeff said. "I saw her driver's license when we did the hiring paperwork. But whatever happened, she's very private about it."

"Hang on," Dawson said. It was his turn to order at the drive-thru. He put in his order, then said, "So, bottom line, she's not dating anyone, but she's not interested either?"

"I've heard her turn down plenty of dates," Jeff said. "But none of them were a tenacious lawyer who can talk a judge and jury into seeing his side of a case."

Dawson chuckled. "Perhaps I do have something going for me."

"You're free to try," Jeff said. "Like I said, don't come crying to me when she turns you down."

"As long as you don't have an issue with me asking her out."

"Go for it," Jeff said. "It will be entertaining on my behalf. If I was a betting man, I'd make some money."

"Keep your money," Dawson said. "But you're going to owe me dinner." After he hung up with Jeff and paid for his meal at the drive-thru window, Dawson drove the rest of the way home, wondering if Clara liked symphony music.

Three

Clara loved Saturday mornings at the real estate office. It was strange, because she never thought she'd want to work on a Saturday. But there was something different about the day, and she always felt revitalized.

Since Saturday was one of their busiest days of the week, as far as Jeff showing clients and answering phone calls, Clara made sure to get to the office early. As usual, she had the coffee pot going by eight. And by nine, she'd already drilled through quite a few inquiries that had come in overnight. It seemed that Friday night was a popular time to browse real estate listings.

By ten, she was pouring her second cup of coffee and debating if she should make a run to the Main Street Café and bring in muffins. A potential client, Mr. and Mrs. Tuttle, said they'd be stopping by the office to meet with Jeff.

Clara sent a text to Jeff about the appointment, and then she grabbed her purse. She'd leave the office open, since she'd only be gone a few minutes.

The café was a half block away, and the cool March morning felt good against her skin. She stifled a yawn and wished she had slept better last night. In fact, she was surprised she hadn't. Usually on yoga nights, she slept longer and more deeply.

But she'd awakened several times, thinking about the yoga class and how Dawson Harris had introduced himself. And how she'd disappeared as soon as she could. Dawson Harris was the last man she could let herself be attracted to. He was Jeff's lawyer, and now that she'd met Dawson in person, not only did he have a girlfriend, but it was clear he was one of those guys who probably had women ogle him everywhere he went.

And Clara refused to join the masses. She kind of wished Dawson would have been less . . . good-looking? Less friendly?

After months of turning down any man who'd asked her out, or hinted at asking her out, she was attracted to her boss's lawyer? She didn't know anything about Dawson's relationship history, but since he was obviously dating Leslie, Clara might have to rethink going to that particular yoga class.

Clara's phone rang just as she reached the café. "Hi, Jeff," she answered before stepping inside. She stepped to the side of the doors as someone passed her by and went into the café.

"I'm going to be about ten minutes late to the appointment with the Tuttles," he said. "Can you grab some muffins from the café?"

"Already on it," Clara said with a laugh.

"Of course you are," Jeff said, his warm voice coming through. "Thanks, Clara. I don't know what I'd do without you."

Clara smiled. It was nice to be appreciated, and it was in moments like this that she wanted to be the best employee ever. If Jeff Finch hadn't hired her, who knew where her life would have ended up? Pine Valley had given her the new start she needed.

"Oh, by the way," Jeff continued. "Dawson said he met you last night."

"Yeah," Clara said, her mind racing. What had Dawson said about her to Jeff? Did they usually hang out on Friday nights? "He came to my yoga class. His girlfriend's the instructor."

"Girlfriend?" Jeff said. "Dawson doesn't have a girlfriend."

Clara's face heated. "Well, whatever. I just thought that he and Leslie were . . . never mind." *Dawson doesn't have a girlfriend* kept running through her mind. "Do you want me to get anything besides muffins?"

"Um, donut holes?" Jeff said. "Clara, I just need to tell you something before the day gets away from me. And you can take this however you want, but when Dawson called me last night, he asked if you had a boyfriend."

All the air seemed to leave Clara's body, and she against the outside wall of the café.

"Make of it what you will," Jeff continued. "But since you're my employee, and I don't want to lose you for any reason, I don't want you to feel like you have to go out with Dawson if he asks you. I mean, he can be fairly, uh, persuasive, but lawyers are a dime a dozen. Good office managers aren't."

Clara inhaled. She was still breathing, apparently. "Thanks for the heads-up," she finally said. "I'm not really interested in dating right now. I'm sort of on a break."

"I get it," Jeff said. "Dawson's been a tremendous help to

me, but I don't want you to feel uncomfortable in any way while working for me. So if I have to, I'll hire another lawyer."

"No, that's a bit drastic," Clara said. "I mean, it's not like he's calling me to ask me out, or anything."

When Jeff didn't respond, Clara said, "What else did he ask?"

"Just what I told you," Jeff said. "But I could hear the interest in his voice. He's been through a recent divorce, and his mom keeps trying to set him up on dates, but from what I know, he's not dating anyone. Dawson is an extremely busy man, and he's never called me for any personal reason. Until last night."

Clara let that sink in. "Okay," she said with what she hoped sounded like a breezy voice. "Like I said, thanks for the heads-up. And just so you know, Jeff, I love my job, and I'm grateful that you hired me."

"Believe me, you've been a godsend," he said. "Especially since I've been dealing with this lawsuit. And you've put in a ton of extra hours. Don't think I haven't noticed."

Clara nodded, even though Jeff couldn't see it. "No problem." After they hung up, she waited a moment, collecting her thoughts, before she entered the café. Jeff was an amazing guy, a great boss, and if there was any attraction between them, she'd probably be a blushing mess. But, although Jeff was close to her age, and a very nice-looking man, there was nothing between them.

On the other hand . . . Dawson had asked if she had a boyfriend. Clara was having a hard time comprehending that Dawson Harris would call up Jeff after the yoga class and ask about her. Yes, they'd had several conversations over the phone, but they'd never talked about anything beyond Jeff or business. Their conversations had been light, friendly, and Clara had never felt like he was flirting.

But now, knowing that Dawson had called Jeff last night to specifically ask about her, she was suddenly nervous. What if he called the office again and she answered? She'd probably sound like an awkward teenager.

Clara exhaled and moved to the doors of the café. She entered the restaurant and placed her order. She had to refocus her thoughts. She already knew that if Dawson asked her out, she'd turn him down. She wasn't ready to trust guys, not yet. The night Max had broken off their engagement still seemed like a horrible dream—but it had been real. Having the man you were in love with confess that he'd fallen in love with his co-worker, and that they'd been seeing each other for over a year, had ripped out Clara's heart.

She'd felt such the fool. She'd felt like a piece of discarded trash.

The only thing good that came of that horrible night was that after crying half the night, she'd called in sick to work and gone back to bed. If she hadn't been home, she wouldn't have been there when her grandma collapsed in the kitchen. Clara wouldn't have been there to call 911 and get her grandma to the hospital. And even though her grandma had never recovered, Clara would have never forgiven herself if she hadn't been home to call the paramedics.

"Clara?" someone called out.

Her order was ready, and she stepped forward to collect the box of muffins and donut holes. She hurried back to the office; she'd been gone much longer than planned. She wanted everything set up before the Tuttles arrived.

Once she had the mini breakfast arranged, she returned to her laptop and continued answering e-mail inquiries about various properties. At the end of each e-mail, she always included the invitation to stop by the realtor office and meet

Jeff in person. Jeff had a natural charisma that put clients at ease, and his laid-back approach didn't make them feel pressured to make quick decisions.

With the Tuttles coming soon, Clara knew the rest of the day would fly by, so she took a couple of guilty moments and googled "Dawson Harris lawyer Pine Valley." Several hits came up, the top one belonging to his law firm. Clara clicked on the link, telling herself she was only doing a professional search. It wasn't like she'd look him up on Facebook or Instagram.

His picture was the top one under the "Our Lawyers" drop-down menu. There he was. Dark-brown eyes, nice smile, hair more neat than it had been at the yoga class.

Clara exhaled and read through the bio. He'd gotten his law degree from Berkeley. Well, then. What was he doing in small-town Pine Valley? She guessed him to be at least thirty, with all the credentials that made up his bio. To stay fair and objective, Clara read through some of the other lawyers' bios. All of them mentioned families, wives, or wives and kids. Dawson's didn't mention anything about his family.

Okay, Clara was getting way too curious. She was already wondering what his ex-wife was like. Why had they gotten divorced? And . . . did he have any kids?

The front door of the office opened, and Clara looked up to see a man walk in, then hold the door open for a woman who must be his wife.

They looked to be in their sixties, and Clara welcomed them inside. "Jeff Finch will be here in about ten minutes," she said, waving them toward the breakfast foods. "Help yourself to muffins and coffee." Her phone started ringing, and Clara answered it.

The rest of the morning and afternoon proved busy, with Jeff meeting with clients and Clara manning the phones. It wasn't until about 3:00 p.m., when Jeff left for a showing, that Clara finally caught a breather. And she was starving.

She set a sign in the window that read "Be back in 20 minutes," then walked to the Main Street Café to grab a sandwich. The line wasn't too long, and she only had to wait a few minutes for her ham and Swiss on wheat. As she walked back to the office, she sipped her lemonade and ate the sandwich. She was too hungry to wait.

She realized someone was standing by the door as she neared the office. She had been gone less than twenty minutes, so she was glad whoever it was had waited.

But as she neared, she realized the man waiting wasn't necessarily a real-estate client. If she had to guess, the man was Dawson Harris. Was he looking for Jeff? Why wouldn't he just call the office or try Jeff's cell? He'd never come to the office before that she knew of. The man turned as she approached.

Yep. *Dawson Harris.* He was wearing dark-gray dress slacks, a button-down shirt, and a tie. Not really Saturday work attire, but maybe lawyers never dressed down, unless they were in a yoga class. The thought made Clara's skin warm. They hadn't even talked yet, and she was on the verge of blushing. Jeff's words ran through her mind as she remembered him telling her how Dawson had asked if she had a boyfriend.

Clara wished she had a free hand to make sure her flyaway hair wasn't too crazy. She'd pulled it back in a clip this morning, but she could feel that strands had come loose about her face and neck.

Taking a deep breath, and pasting on a friendly smile, Clara decided to not let this encounter be as awkward as last night's. So what if he'd called Jeff after the yoga class and asked about her? Clara wasn't ready to date.

"Hello," Clara said before Dawson could speak. "Jeff's out with a client."

"The rest of the day?" he asked.

"I think so," Clara said. "I can double check if you want." So, he was looking for Jeff. Of course he was. What did she expect? She slipped the drink into the crook of her arm so she could unlock the office door with her key. Instead of waiting for her to open the door, Dawson leaned over and opened it for her.

"Oh, thank you," Clara said in her most cheerful tone. Dawson smelled good. Like some sort of spicy cologne. She tried to ignore the way he smelled, and the fact that he'd followed her into the office space.

Clara crossed to her desk and set her sandwich and drink down. She was sure she smelled like ham and cheese and hoped Dawson wouldn't stay too long.

When she turned to see him, he was just standing there, as if waiting for her to look at him before he spoke. She suddenly wanted to hurry to the bathroom to check her makeup and hair, which was ridiculous. Last night she'd been in workout clothes, sweating, and wearing no makeup.

Presently, she was wearing black leggings, an oversized blue sweater, and low-heeled boots. Not too dressy, but not sloppy either. She held up her cell phone. "Do you want me to see if Jeff's coming back?"

"No," Dawson said, slipping his hands into the pockets of his pants. He wasn't carrying a briefcase or manila folders—isn't that what lawyers carried around all the time?

All she knew was that the intensity of his brown eyes focused on her made it hard for her to think straight. She wished he would have just called, although she didn't know if that would have been much better. She felt hyperaware of every action and every word.

"I'm not here to talk to Jeff," Dawson continued.

He seemed so serious that Clara wondered if there was something else wrong. Maybe there was some secret lawsuit against her that he'd been notified of? Maybe the sale of her grandma's house wasn't going to go through after all, and he was here to tell her. None of that made sense, and Clara decided she needed to sit down. But would it be rude to take her place behind her desk before she found out what he wanted?

"Okay, no problem," Clara said, her pulse racing. "Is there something I can help you with, then?"

Dawson smiled. "I hope so. Do you like classical music?"

Four

Dawson wasn't exactly encouraged when Clara's eyes widened at his question. He supposed that asking her if she liked classical music was sort of out-of-the-blue. But he hadn't wanted to call her to see if he still got the same vibe as he did last night—something propelled him to talk to her in person again. Clara was a pretty woman, but she seemed to not realize it at all.

Dawson had slept more poorly than usual last night, waking up several times with his thoughts on Clara, so he'd spent time this morning googling her name and checking out her social media profiles.

He'd made a couple of deductions from all his searching. It looked like she and her former boyfriend were history, and she used to live in Sacramento with her grandma. Her profile said she used to work at an elementary school, but he didn't know if she was a teacher or maybe an office manager.

He decided that if she didn't have a boyfriend, and if Jeff's assessment that she wasn't dating anyone was correct, then Dawson would take the plunge. He'd ask her to the symphony and fill the tickets his mom had told him about. A double date with his parents probably wasn't the ideal first date, but it would certainly test Clara's possible interest.

Since Clara hadn't said anything for a moment, he said, "If you don't like classical music, you won't offend me. I was just wondering."

She took a breath, and Dawson kept his focus on her eyes—which were the exact shade of her blue sweater.

"I—I guess I've never really thought about it," Clara said. "I mean, I just listen to whatever's on the radio. In college I took a humanities class, and we studied classical music."

Dawson nodded. He was glad she'd lost the deer-in-the-headlights look. "So, what did you think? Any favorite composers? Vivaldi? Schubert? Mendelssohn?"

She took a step back and leaned against the desk behind her. "Um, not really. I can barely remember any of their names."

"But you weren't averse to them?"

"Averse?"

"You didn't hate the music?"

She straightened and folded her arms. "I know what *averse* means, Mr. Harris."

Dawson lifted his hands. He hadn't meant to make her defensive. "Okay, look," he said, deciding to get right to the point. "My mom has four tickets to the symphony tomorrow night. She and my dad are going, and they invited me. Told me to bring a date. I thought I'd invite you to come along . . . as my date."

Clara's mouth fell open. Her defensiveness melted away, and she stared at him, a pink blush on her cheeks. "You're . . ." Her voice trailed off.

"And maybe you can call me Dawson?" he said, smiling.

Clara bit her lip, and Dawson's smile dropped. She was going to turn him down. He knew it. Jeff had known it. He'd warned Dawson. Once Jeff heard about this, he'd have a good laugh.

"Dawson, I don't really know you," she said in a hesitant voice. "I think you're a . . ." She unfolded her arms and waved her hand.

What did the hand wave mean?

"You're a . . ." She was biting her lip again.

Now, Dawson felt like an idiot. He'd never been rejected to his face, and his ex-wife didn't count. Maybe he should have called Clara instead. Was she going to tell him to get out of the office? To never speak to her again? He knew without a doubt that Jeff would totally take her side.

"I'm what?" Dawson finally prompted.

"Sort of . . ." She took a step forward, her chin lifted. "I don't mean to offend you, Mr. Harris, but you're sort of overwhelming. And I'm not interested in dating anyone, so please don't take offense."

Dawson exhaled. "I'm not offended that you're not interested in dating, but I'm not sure what you mean by 'overwhelming.'"

She released a half-laugh that wasn't really joyful. "You're the top lawyer in Pine Valley, you're charismatic, sophisticated, and you're a good-looking guy. You wear ties on the weekend. You walk into a yoga class and are better than everyone who's been there for months. You go to symphonies. You know the difference between classical music composers. On my days off, I'm more likely to go on a hike, have a peanut butter sandwich while reading a cheesy romance novel. My dates are more along the lines of pizza and Netflix."

Dawson wanted to laugh about the picnic and cheesy romance novel, but he was pretty sure she was dead serious. "You think I'm good-looking?"

Clara put her hands on her hips. "As if you don't know that."

"How would *I* know what you're thinking?" he countered.

She seemed to hesitate. "I'm like many other women who notice a handsome man. There are plenty of them around, and you're one of them. But that's not my point. You and I are just too different."

"Of course we're different." Dawson didn't know whether to laugh or to be annoyed. He took a step closer, which meant she had to look up more to hold his gaze. "I'm a man, you're a woman. That's pretty different."

She blinked, and Dawson wondered if she wore contacts. He'd never seen eyes such a deep blue as hers.

Clara didn't move or back down, and this Dawson liked. A lot. His ex-wife would have never argued with him. If she didn't agree with him, she'd just shut down and give him the silent treatment. They hadn't even argued about their divorce. She'd moved out while he was at work, and he was served divorce papers at his office.

"I'm tall, and you're kind of short," he continued, looking down at Clara. He had the urge to smooth back a few strands of her auburn hair that had escaped her hair clip. "You have red hair and—"

"Okay, I get it!" she said, but there was amusement in her eyes.

"I think differences are good," Dawson said. "I mean, it makes things more interesting, don't you agree?" He could see that he was starting to win her over. She seemed to be considering his side of the argument.

She smiled.

He felt like doing a victory dance.

"Nice try, Mr. Harris," she said. "I know Jeff thinks highly of you, and that you're probably a good lawyer. You're probably great with the ladies, too, but I'm just not interested."

He wanted to keep arguing, because he could see in her eyes that she *was* interested. But he had some pride left. If there was one thing his divorce taught him, it was to know when he had lost. "All right, no problem. If you change your mind, you have my number."

She arched a single brow. "I do."

"Okay, then," Dawson said. "I hope you have a nice weekend." He turned away then, because it was really the only thing he could do and still maintain his dignity.

As he stepped out onto the street, he was grateful for the cool breeze that had kicked up. He loosened the knot on his tie and thought about the irony of life. Leslie was constantly asking him to do this and that, and he turned her down all the time. And now that he was truly interested in getting to know another woman, *she'd* turned *him* down.

Dawson walked the few yards to where he'd parked his truck. He jumped in, thinking that today would just be like every other weekend, where he'd work straight through. It was no big deal; it was what he'd been doing for years. It was part of why he was now divorced. There was always one more thing to research, one more client to call, one more brief to review.

But right now, he didn't want to do any of it. For the first time in a long time, he could care less about staying at the top of his game. He wanted to turn off his cell and disconnect from everything for a while.

Eighteen hours later, he still hadn't turned off his cell, because what if Clara changed her mind? Not about the symphony; it was too late for that. He'd told his mom he couldn't make it at all—date or no date. She'd tried to talk him into taking Paula Smith, of course, but Dawson didn't feel like putting on pretenses. Especially for a single mom with two kids. Even though his history with Paula wasn't all that positive, she didn't deserve to be caught in the middle of his mom's matchmaking schemes.

Besides, he kept thinking about what Clara had told him about their differences—aside from the obvious ones. Did he come across as "overwhelming"? He certainly hoped he did in a court room, but maybe he should tone it down outside of the courtroom. The question was *how*? Order pizza and binge-watch Netflix? He had a feeling he'd lose thousands of brain cells if he did. Read romance novels? He laughed.

Then he paused. He could at least read something other than legal documents. Maybe he could run to the bookstore on Main Street and get a paperback. He hadn't read anything other than what was necessary work for years.

An hour later, he found himself at the bookstore, browsing the newest releases. A romance cover caught his eye—it wasn't one of those bodice rippers... at least, the hero and heroine were fully clothed.

"Can I help you?" an employee asked.

Dawson looked up to see a young brunette with purple-rimmed glasses. Her name tag read: *Felicity.* Before he asked her his question, he glanced about the store. Only two other people were inside browsing, but they were out of earshot. "What are some of the top-selling romances you carry?"

Credit went to the employee when she didn't gasp or even raise an eyebrow. She pointed to one of the books on the display table. "Rachael Anderson's books are really popular. She writes wholesome romances, both contemporary and Regency."

Dawson gazed at the cover—the woman was wearing an old-fashioned dress. "What do you mean by *Regency*?"

"Oh, it's specific to Regency England, early 1800s, during the rule of the Prince Regent," she said.

It all went over his head, but he picked up the book anyway and started to thumb through it. An idea was forming in his head.

"If your girlfriend or wife likes to read historical romance, she'll like Rachael's books," she continued. "They're sweet and clean."

Dawson frowned. "What do you mean by 'clean'?"

"No sex scenes."

Dawson swallowed, his throat suddenly dry. He didn't correct the employee on the girlfriend/wife assumption. "All right. I'll get it. Anything else you recommend?"

"In romances?"

He nodded. His face also might have been turning red.

"Sure, there's a new contemporary romance by Amy Harmon out," she said. "We have a stack of them by the register."

Two romances sounded like a decent start, and Dawson followed the employee to the register. Moments later he left the bookstore, not entirely sure he could believe that he'd just purchased two romance novels.

Five

"It's not a problem," Clara told Jeff Finch over the phone. It was a rainy Monday, which pretty much matched her mood. And now Jeff was calling into work sick, which meant she'd be spending the next hour rescheduling all his appointments for today, and possibly tomorrow. "I hope you feel better soon. Do you want me to bring you soup or anything?"

He chuckled, which quickly turned into a deep cough. "Uh, my mom has that one covered," he said when he could talk again. "Thanks for the offer, though. I'll let you know if I'm feeling better tomorrow."

"Sounds good," Clara said, leaning back in her office chair. She was glad Jeff was taking the day off. He sounded terrible, and she didn't want to catch whatever he had.

"Oh, one more thing," Jeff said, his voice scratchy.

"What is it?" She'd already written down about seven tasks Jeff had rattled off when she'd first answered her phone.

"I thought I'd give you a little heads-up in case you're interested," he continued.

"What's going on?"

"Well, yesterday I ran into Dawson Harris when I was out doing errands."

Clara stiffened. She'd tried not to feel guilty about turning down Dawson's invitation for a date. She might have eaten a little too much chocolate over the weekend, but tonight at yoga, she was determined to cleanse her thoughts and move forward. Yeah, Dawson was a good-looking man, and charming, but she stuck by all she'd told him. Their differences were too great.

No, things hadn't worked out with Max, even though they'd had a lot in common, but that was in the past. And Clara wanted to be one-hundred percent Clara before she started dating again. She braced herself for what Jeff might say next.

"Well, I noticed he'd bought some books, and when I asked him what he was reading, I'll just have to say, I was shocked."

Clara had no idea where Jeff was going with this. She didn't really want to talk about Dawson Harris anyway.

"You won't believe this, but he'd bought two romance novels—for *himself*. He said he was expanding his reading arsenal. Of course I gave him plenty of crap." Jeff laughed, which turned into another coughing fit.

"That's pretty crazy," Clara said, her thoughts spinning.

"Anyway, thought you'd get a kick out of that," Jeff said. "I guess everyone has strange quirks. Hey, did he ever call you?"

"No. No, he didn't," Clara said quickly. It seemed that

Dawson Harris hadn't told Jeff that he'd asked her out, so she decided she'd keep it to herself. Dawson hadn't *called* her either, so it wasn't like she was lying to her boss.

Jeff cleared his throat. "Okay, I'd better go. I think my mom's here with that soup. Thanks, Clara."

She hung up with Jeff and stared out the office windows. The rain was coming down hard. Maybe Dawson had bought the romance novels for his mom or someone else. But she had a feeling that he'd bought them because of their argument on Saturday. She shook her head—was he really going to read romances?

She wondered which ones he'd bought, and then she found herself smiling about it. Dawson Harris was a pretty stubborn guy. That probably served him well in court.

The sound of a cat meowing distracted Clara. She fed a stray cat occasionally in the parking lot behind the building, but the cat meowing at the door was an entirely new thing.

She went to the back door and cracked it open.

Sure enough, there was the scruffy calico cat, huddled underneath the awning. "Hang on," Clara said with a laugh. "I'll get you something to eat."

But then the cat came through the doorway and headed straight for the door to the storage room. Clara opened that, too, and scooped out a bowl of from the cat food bag she kept there. She suspected Jeff had also fed the cat from time to time. Had he let it inside before? She set the bowl on the ground to let the cat eat, then left the storage room door open.

The office phone started to ring, so she went to answer it. She answered the questions from a potential client as best she could, but she was no Jeff Finch. So in the end, she said she'd have Jeff Finch call the lady back when he was feeling better.

After the phone call, Clara went to check the cat. It had curled up on top of a closed box of brochures and was asleep.

"Okay, then," Clara whispered. "When it stops raining, you're going back outside." She felt sorry for the poor thing, but she couldn't take it home because her apartment had a no-pet rule.

The driving rain was keeping walk-in customers out, and within the next hour, Clara had caught up on all the emails that had come in over the weekend. Curious, she pulled up the spreadsheet of Jeff's contacts and found Dawson's numbers. Both an office number and cell number were listed.

Clara knew that if she reached out to Dawson Harris, she'd be changing up everything she'd told him. Yet, it wasn't as if she was asking him on a date, right? Maybe she could just tease him a little . . . he *had* bought romance novels.

She put his cell number into her own cell phone. Then, after debating another ten minutes, she finally texted him: *Jeff told me about your eclectic reading choices. I was surprised.* She hit SEND, then held her breath. Good thing she didn't hold her breath for long, because Dawson didn't reply.

In fact, two more hours passed, and with each passing minute, Clara felt smaller and smaller. And dumb. And silly. He was probably really busy. Maybe even in court. *She* was the one who had turned him down flat for a date. A man like Dawson Harris likely didn't give second chances. Was she playing games? No. Just as she'd told him, they were different. Very different. But maybe he'd really listened to her, and that's why he'd bought the books, and maybe . . .

Her phone rang, and her heart nearly stopped when she saw *Dawson Harris* appear on the incoming call. He hadn't texted her back . . . He was *calling* her.

Clara let it ring once, then twice . . . her pulse was now racing like crazy . . . *third ring.* She answered, hoping she sounded cool.

"Was it a good surprise or bad surprise?" he said with no preamble.

The tones of his low voice coming through the phone seemed to melt into her. "Depends on the books," she said.

Dawson laughed. It was a nice laugh. One that reached to her toes.

"Oh really?" he said. "All right. For your information, although it's technically none of your business, since you don't want to hang out with me, I got *The Pursuit of Lady Harriett* by Rachael Anderson, and *The Smallest Part* by Amy Harmon."

"Wow," Clara said. "I'm impressed. I've read the *Lady Harriett* book, but not Amy Harmon's yet."

"Want to borrow it when I'm done?" he asked.

Clara smiled. "Maybe. And I didn't say I didn't want to hang out with you."

Dawson seemed to pause at this.

Clara knew she'd just thrown him a pretty big lead. She'd be interested to see what his lawyer-mind came back with.

"You're right," he said. "You didn't say those words exactly, but you did turn me down when I asked you out on a date."

"With your *parents*," she said. "I mean, no woman in her right mind would have said yes to a first date that involves parents."

"Very true," Dawson said, and she swore she could hear the smile in his voice. "That was extremely poor form. You know, if the problem was the parent thing, I can definitely remedy that."

She closed her eyes. Here it came.

"Except you said you didn't want to date," Dawson continued.

Clara felt her heart sink. He had a good memory and was

good about dissecting their previous conversation. She *had* told him she didn't want to date. And for very good reasons . . . except she couldn't remember what they were now.

"So, I was thinking," he said in that deep voice of his. "We could *hang* out. Maybe at a restaurant. Around dinner time? Absolutely no parents allowed."

Clara laughed.

"We could discuss romance novels," Dawson continued, his tone hopeful.

"Tell you what, Mr. Harris," Clara said. "Read one of those books, and then maybe we'll hang out."

He didn't say anything for a moment, and she wished she could see his face.

"I think I'm starting to like how you call me *Mr. Harris,*" he said in a low voice. "It's Regency-like."

"You already started reading it?" she asked.

"I did. And I can see how I need to earn the right for you to call me by my first name," he said. "Should I be calling you Miss Benson?"

Clara smiled. "Clara is fine."

"All right, Clara," he continued. "Keep your nights free. I should be finished with both of these books in no time."

Clara's pulse was racing again by the time she'd hung up with Dawson. He had done the unexpected, and she probably shouldn't let it sway her, but she had. She closed her eyes and exhaled. Was she ready for this? Probably not. Maybe when he called her again, she'd have more resolve to turn him down.

That thought gave her comfort, but she also suspected she had a dinner date in her near future. Dawson didn't seem like the kind of man who would go back on a promise. Which made him different than Max.

The rain never let up, and since the office was so slow, she downloaded the Amy Harmon book to her Kindle app and started to read. If she and Dawson did end up having dinner together, she'd know if he was bluffing.

Six

"I'm finished," Dawson said as soon as Clara answered her phone. Reading have two books over four nights had been a feat, and he might have only slept three hours last night, but he hoped it would be worth it.

"With the Regency?" Clara asked, amusement in her tone.

"With both." He waited for it.

"Are you serious?" she said, then laughed. "You are one determined man, Mr. Harris."

"That's both a strength and a weakness." He rested his head against the headrest in his truck. It had been a crazy day at the office, and he'd fielded several calls from new clients, as well as tried to get schedules coordinated for upcoming court dates. One of the cases had a prosecutor whom Dawson always clashed with. Since Dawson had won the last several cases against this particular prosecutor, things were strained between them.

Even with all the busyness of today, he'd managed to read the final two chapters of Harmon's book over lunch. He'd eaten a Subway sandwich at his desk, with the door shut, as he read. He had to maintain some sort of dignity.

He and Clara had texted a few times over the past four days. It had taken a lot of will power not to call her, but now that he had, he decided to feel flattered she'd answered on the first ring.

Tomorrow he'd be in court most of the day, and depending on the outcome, he could be in a foul mood. So his goal was to get Clara to agree to meet him for dinner tonight... or their non-date would have to wait until Saturday night.

"What did you think?" Clara asked, genuine interest in her tone.

"Oh, no you don't," he said. "You have to wait until our date, I mean, our *hang-out session*, to find out my thoughts."

She laughed. "I see what you're doing."

He loved the way she laughed. "Hungry?"

"Maybe."

"You would be a terrible witness if you ever had to testify in a court case," Dawson said. "It's a simple yes-or-no question. Either you're hungry or you're not."

"Hmmm," she started. "I'm not sure I agree. Sometimes I'm a little hungry, and I only need a granola bar. Or, I'm very hungry, and I need a full meal, and maybe dessert. Other times, I just crave something sweet—like ice cream or chocolate."

"Okay, I concede," Dawson said with a laugh. "Are you a little hungry, *very* hungry, or craving ice cream or chocolate?"

Clara only paused for a second. "I'm very hungry."

Warmth spread through Dawson. Now they were getting somewhere. "Great. Can I pick you up, or is that breaking your hang-out rules? We could meet at a restaurant. Have you been to Rick's BBQ? They have salads, too, not that I'm expecting you to order a salad."

"I like salad, and ribs." Clara released a small sigh. "Do you want to pick me up at the office? I live in the opposite direction."

Dawson felt like he'd just been awarded a gold star. "Sure, when are you done?"

"I'm done, but I can always work on stuff until you get here."

"I can be there in about fifteen minutes."

Dawson hung up with Clara and started his truck. He wouldn't have time to go home and change, so he just tugged off his tie, unbuttoned his cuffs, and rolled up his sleeves. He'd take the grief if she gave it to him. It would be worth every minute.

As he headed toward Main Street and the realty office, he tried to remember the last time he'd felt so eager for a date. Had he felt this way when he'd been dating Romy? They had started dating in college, and it just seemed that everyone expected them to be together. So when she'd become pregnant during their last year of college, they married. Later, she'd had a miscarriage, but Dawson had thought their marriage was still worth it. She worked as a dental hygienist while he went to law school. His hours were long, and late, but that was how law school was. Romy had always been quiet, yet she'd had a decent circle of girlfriends. When he'd received the divorce papers, she had included a three-page, single-spaced letter, laying down all of her feelings—which amounted to a giant list of his failures—all things she'd never told him in six years of marriage.

Dawson pulled his truck up to the curb in front of the realty office. He had just climbed out when Clara came out of the front door of the office. Her auburn hair hung straight, just below her shoulders, and she wore navy dress pants with a pale blue blouse. The blouse was fairly sheer, and underneath she seemed to be wearing a dark blue tank shirt. He pulled his gaze away from her outfit to meet her amused gaze.

"Got rid of your tie, did you?" she asked.

Dawson smiled. "I didn't want to upstage my date, I mean, my hang-out buddy."

Clara smirked, and she glanced over at the truck. "Well, I wasn't expecting you to drive a truck."

He arched his brows. "What did you expect?"

Clara looked Dawson up and down. "Mercedes? Or maybe a BMW?"

Dawson motioned to the truck. "You would be wrong, Miss Benson."

She shook her head but was smiling. He moved to the passenger door and opened it for her.

"Thank you, sir," she said as she climbed in.

Dawson could swear he smelled citrus. He had the sudden urge to tug her toward him so he could breathe in the scent of her hair. Instead, he shut her door after she was settled and walked around the front of the truck.

When he climbed in and started his truck, Clara said, "This reminds me of my grandpa. He had a red truck, and he babied it. I remember my grandma telling me she was sometimes jealous of it."

Dawson chuckled. "That's sort of ironic, because my grandpa had a truck too. It looks like we do have something in common."

"Wow, that's unexpected," she said, clipping on her seatbelt.

"My grandpa's truck wasn't red, but we used to go fishing together," he said as he pulled out onto Main. "I always felt like such a big kid because he'd let me ride up front. There weren't airbags back then."

"The good old days," Clara said. "Is your grandpa still around?"

"No," he said. "He died when I was sixteen. How about your grandparents?"

Clara sighed and looked out her window. "My grandma died a few months ago. My grandpa has been gone for about eight years."

"I'm sorry," Dawson said. "Were you close?"

Clara glanced at him, and Dawson wished he wasn't having to drive. He hadn't expected their conversation to take such a serious turn.

"My grandparents raised me," she said. "I never knew my mom. And my dad, well, he struggled with some serious addictions. So my grandparents filed for custody." She waved a hand. "Don't worry. My childhood was great. My grandparents were the best parents a girl could ask for."

Although her tone was light-hearted, Dawson sensed a deep pain there. "Then I'm glad you had your grandparents."

Clara picked up her purse and pulled out a white envelope. "Today I received notice that my grandma's house is under contract. It's kind of crazy to think about. When she died, my life was a pretty big mess, so my solution was to start over. Somewhere. Pine Valley was the lucky destination. But, I always knew my home—my grandma's home—was still there, waiting for me. Now, it won't be."

Her voice trembled at the last sentence, and Dawson reached over and squeezed her hand as he slowed the truck to stop at a traffic light. "We don't have to go to Rick's BBQ if you don't want to."

"No, it's okay," Clara said, taking a shaky breath. "Life happens, and I'd rather be with someone than alone right now."

Her eyes were bluer than blue, Dawson decided. She pulled her hand from beneath his.

"Don't let it go to your head, though," Clara said, giving him a tremulous smile.

Dawson returned the smile. "I'll try not to, but I can't promise anything."

Clara slid the envelope back into her purse.

The traffic light changed to green, so Dawson stepped on the accelerator.

After a moment of silence, Dawson ventured, "What was your grandma like?"

"Oh," she said with a half-laugh, "she was a homemaker through and through. Made everything from scratch. Kept the house pristine. She fussed over everything, but I adored her for it."

"She sounds pretty amazing."

"Yeah, she was amazing," Clara said. "Every day before I left for work, she said, 'Say you love me.' It was sort of our thing."

Dawson smiled. "My grandpa used to make me guess between numbers one through ten. If I guessed right, he'd take me fishing." He felt Clara's gaze on him.

"I'll bet you were a sad little boy if you guessed wrong," she said.

He shrugged. "No matter what number I guessed, he said I was always right." He laughed. "I never knew which number he had in mind. He just pretended whatever I said was that number."

"Grandparents are the best," Clara said in a wistful tone.

They'd arrived at the restaurant, and Dawson pulled into

the parking lot and stopped. Before he shut off the ignition, he looked over at Clara. "Will you be all right? We can do something else if you want."

One side of her mouth lifted as her gaze met him. Dawson knew he could get lost in her blue eyes pretty easily. "Are you trying to get out of our book discussion?"

Dawson lifted his hands from the steering wheel. "Never."

Clara's lips lifted into a full smile. "Then, let's go. I'm starving."

Seven

Clara kept catching Dawson looking at her. "You know, a lady doesn't like to be stared at," she told him. "Especially when she's eating."

Dawson only grinned. "I've just never had a date enjoy her food so much. Please, continue." He slid the giant platter of ribs toward her.

"Ha. Ha." The truth was that Dawson had already eaten most of what they'd ordered. Clara was a slower eater, and she was only on her fourth rib. "So, what did you like best about the books you read?"

"Can I tell you what I hated first?" Dawson said. "I want to get that part out of the way."

"All right." Clara couldn't wait to hear what he thought about the romance novels. She knew she was allowing herself to be captivated by this man, but she was enjoying every minute with him. It surprised her. She didn't want to overthink it.

"First, I hated the fact that you told me I had to read them before you'd hang out with me," he said. "That made me feel like I was doing homework or something."

She took another bite of her food, hiding her smile.

"Then, I hated that I couldn't complain to someone while I was reading," he said. "I just had to accept everything and continue reading. I couldn't change anything in the story."

Clara wiped her mouth with her napkin, then said, "What do you mean?"

"In the legal world, everything is questioned and analyzed." He picked up his glass and took a drink. "I couldn't argue with anything going on."

She laughed. "Surely you've read novels before."

"Yeah, some in high school," he said. "Those classic kinds."

She had a hard-time picturing this man sitting on a couch reading *Of Mice and Men* or *The Scarlet Letter*. He looked like he'd spent most of his time on the basketball court or football field. "What else did you hate about the plots you had no control over?"

"I hated the miscommunication," he said. "I mean, if men and women just told each other what they were thinking, so much angst could be avoided. But maybe that's the lawyer in me talking. I'd much rather see an argument play out, rather than a resulting crime committed."

Clara stared at him. "I think you're onto something. But people are afraid to say what they really think."

"Why be afraid?" Dawson said. "If my ex-wife had told me what she was really feeling during our marriage, we'd probably still be married."

"She didn't talk to you?"

"Not about what she really thought," he said. "Instead of telling me, her husband, that she was unhappy with our marriage and life together, she put it all in a letter with the divorce papers."

Clara knew it wasn't her business to know what was in the letter from his ex-wife, so she asked, "Did you always tell her what *you* felt or thought?"

"Within reason," Dawson said, his tone lightening a little. "I mean, there are things you never tell a woman. Or your wife. Like, you never comment on her weight or appearance or compliment another woman around her."

"True," Clara said. "But you had no trouble commenting on my eating habits."

He laughed, and it was good to hear, Clara decided. Something in her heart had tugged when Dawson spoke of his divorce. She could see that the confident, charismatic man had been through some tough trials.

"So, what do you think about being completely honest with each other, right from the beginning?" Dawson said, watching her closely.

Clara wondered if she'd ever get used to this man's close scrutiny. He was a lawyer, so maybe it was in his nature, but he'd also apparently completely missed the boat with his ex-wife. "I think honesty is generally a good policy, but like you said, there are things you don't say to others. Even if it's the truth."

"Because the truth can hurt?" Dawson mused.

"Exactly."

"Okay, I get that, but what if you told me one truth about me . . . just one that you carefully select, but it's the absolute truth."

Clara exhaled. "I'm not sure that's a good thing, Mr. Harris."

He gave her a pleading look. "Humor me."

Clara used one of the moist wipes the waitress had brought to clean off her hands. Then she folded her arms and leaned back. "What sort of truth are we talking about?"

"Let's say . . ." He paused, but Clara knew perfectly well that he'd already thought this all through. "Let's tell each other what our first impressions were of each other when we met at the yoga class. The honest, brutal truth."

Clara covered her mouth and groaned. "I don't think so."

Dawson tilted his head, his eyes flashing with amusement. "Why not?"

"Because, like I said earlier, I don't want your head to get too big."

His eyebrows shot up. "So it was good stuff."

Clara's face warmed.

"All right, all right," he said lifting his hands. "How about I start?"

She exhaled. "I don't know if that would be much better, because then you'll still expect me to tell you what I thought."

He shrugged those broad shoulders of his. "I'm not going to force you to spill your secrets, Miss Benson." Then he winked.

She sighed. "Just get it over with." She wanted to bury her face in her hands, but she held his gaze.

Dawson grinned. "Well, I have to preface this by saying that I'd seen your picture on the website. I won't deny that I thought you were pretty. We'd talked on the phone a few times, and although I thought you were a personable office manager and Jeff was lucky to have you working for him, I also wasn't ready to let my mind go into any sort of direction that might lead to asking you out."

"Because of your divorce?"

"That's what I told myself. But when I met you, that all sort of went out the window," he said.

"What went out of the window?"

"The idea that I wasn't ready to move on, or to try starting over on any level with another woman and possible relationship." Dawson shifted closer in the booth and lowered his voice. "So, when I did see you—meet you in person—I was taken by surprise."

He was close enough that Clara imagined she could feel the warmth coming from his skin.

"What were you surprised about?" Clara prompted when he didn't continue right away. The intensity of his gaze was making her pulse hammer.

"How all my hang-ups seemed to evaporate," he said. "Leslie has been hinting at going out for weeks, and a few other women in my circles. But I'd done everything I could to avoid them or turn them down politely. But when I saw you . . ." His gaze scanned her face, then returned to her eyes. "I knew you were different."

Clara rolled her eyes. "Yeah. *Different.* Like I said."

He leaned toward her, and their arms touched. "Different than any woman I'd met. I can't exactly explain it, but I couldn't stop thinking about you. So, I decided to satisfy my curiosity, and I came to your office to see you in person again. To see if I was still interested enough to ask you out."

"And I turned you down."

"And you turned me down."

Clara swallowed. He smelled good. And he was saying very nice, flattering words.

He raised his brows and quirked his mouth. He was waiting for her.

"Truth?" she said.

"Truth."

"I didn't know who you were at first—since I'd never looked up your firm's website or anything," Clara said. "But when you came into the class, I was very aware of you, just like all of the other women were."

His eyes widened slightly, but he said nothing.

"You can't be surprised," she continued. "I immediately knew you weren't a regular and assumed you were there for Leslie. So I kept my eyes closed and did my best to ignore you."

"Did it work?" he asked.

"It might have worked if you didn't show Jeff those romances you bought."

Dawson's chuckle was low. "But what did you think when we actually *met*?"

The restaurant was feeling a bit warm, so she took another sip of her ice water. "Well . . . I thought you were, uh, handsome. And then I felt a little jealous of Leslie."

A smile played on his lips, and Clara knew she was blushing.

"Don't get all worked up, because there are a lot of men I find attractive," she said. "But I hadn't really expected you to look like you." She waved a hand. "I thought you were already taken, so I just put you out of my mind."

"Hmm," he said, but didn't elaborate.

"Then Jeff called."

Dawson smiled.

Clara took a longer drink of her ice water. "I think that's enough truth for today," she said. "Speaking the truth is harder than it sounds."

He looked reluctant to drop their conversation, but then he said, "Do you want dessert?"

"I couldn't," she said.

"Something to go?"

"No, I'm fine. But you're welcome to order something." She shifted so that she wasn't so close to Dawson.

He signaled the waitress. "We'll take the check, please."

Clara was finally feeling more calm and cool. They were back to reality. Her racing pulse could return to normal. This dinner with Dawson had been nice. But she remembered that she didn't want rose-colored glasses. She'd once thought Max was everything she wanted in a man. So how could she enjoy spending time with someone so different?

When the waitress brought the check, Dawson snatched it.

"If you pay, it will be a date," Clara said, reaching for it.

He held it out of her reach. The only way she could get it was if she climbed over his lap.

"How about I'll pay today," he said. "And you can pay next time."

"Next time?"

"Yeah. I mean, I never told you what I liked about those romances."

Clara folded her arms as he signed the receipt. "You could tell me now."

"Nope." Dawson looked up and smiled.

Why did he have to have such a nice smile?

"I think it would be good for you to be in suspense," he said. "Ready?"

She nodded and scooted out of the booth. Dawson was faster and held out his hand to help her up. She put her hand in his warm one. She withdrew her hand as soon as possible so that he wouldn't think she was going soft on him.

He just chuckled as he motioned for her to lead the way. He was a gentleman.

She found that she was smiling as she walked outside. It

had grown dark, and the air had cooled considerably. She tried not to shiver, but Dawson noticed.

"Cold?" he asked, opening the passenger door of his truck.

"I'll warm up soon enough," she said.

"Here," he said, stepping near her and reaching into the back seat of the truck.

Clara had to lean back so he wouldn't bump into her.

He held up a suit coat. "Put this on."

It would keep her warmer. So with Dawson's help, she slipped her arms into the sleeves, then climbed into the front seat.

Dawson shut the door after her, and as he walked around the truck to the other side, she allowed herself to relish the feeling of wearing his jacket. It smelled like him. Warm and spicy and just . . . Dawson.

Eight

Dawson woke up to light streaming through the blinds in his bedroom. He squinted in the brightness and reached for his cell phone on the bedside table. He flipped it over and saw that it was nine o'clock in the morning. Panic jolted through him, and then he remembered it was Sunday. Technically, he could sleep in. But he couldn't remember sleeping in since high school.

He lay back on his pillows again, the phone still in his hand, as his mind caught up with the events from the last few days. Thursday night he and Clara had gone to Rick's BBQ. Friday he'd won his big court case, getting his client who owned a used car lot the money her ex-husband owed her. He'd come home exhausted, and behind on preparing for Monday. He'd been up until after midnight, then awake again early Saturday.

He'd worked through the entire day, only stopping for an obligatory lunch with his mom. He'd also texted Clara. She'd replied, but everything was short. Dawson decided he didn't like to communicate with Clara through texting. In person was much, much better. Today, he hoped to see her.

But first, he'd need to see if his paralegal had reviewed the documents he'd sent over yesterday. He sat up in bed and pulled up the email app on his phone. Sure enough, there was the file. After a quick shower and something to eat, he'd open it up on his laptop and go over the changes. He typed a thank-you reply, then made his way to the shower.

Fifteen minutes later, he had juice and a bagel sitting on the kitchen counter next to his laptop. He'd just started reading his paralegal's notes when someone knocked at his door. He decided to just ignore it.

Another knock sounded. Then Leslie's voice came through, loud and clear. "I know you're in there, Dawson. Your red truck is a dead giveaway." She laughed.

Dawson stifled a groan, and he walked to the door. Sure enough, through the peephole he could see Leslie, wearing a hot-pink jacket and bouncing up and down.

He turned the dead bolt and opened the door.

"Oh, goodness!" she said, her eyes widening. "You're, uh, not dressed."

Dawson glanced down and realized he wasn't wearing a shirt. Only his gym shorts. He smiled, hoping to pass on the message that he could go shirtless in his own apartment.

"I—I stopped by to invite you to a neighbor lunch," Leslie said, finally meeting his eyes. Her face nearly matched the color of her jacket. "It's just me, you, Tiff, and Robby. You know him, from apartment 3F?"

Vaguely. Dawson scrubbed a hand through his hair. Now that he'd gone to Leslie's yoga class, he felt that he didn't have to play the good-neighbor routine to the extent of having lunch together. "I already have lunch plans, but thanks for the invite."

"Oh? Really?" Leslie gave him a slow smile. "With another woman?"

Dawson could easily bring up his mom at this point, but that wouldn't deter someone like Leslie. She'd probably like him all the more for it. But if he told her he was going out with another woman, specifically Clara, whom Leslie actually knew . . .

"Yes, Clara Benson," he said. "She's in your yoga class."

Leslie's face lost some of its color. "Clara? She's . . . yes, she's in my class." She looked Dawson up and down. "I didn't think she was your type, you know, she's sort of . . ." Leslie pursed her lips.

"Thanks again for the invite," he said and started to close the door.

"Wait!" Leslie shot out her hand to stop the door from closing. "What about later? I mean, maybe just you and I can go on a hike. It's really good for your thigh muscles."

Dawson almost rolled his eyes when she ogled him again. He leaned against the door frame. "I don't think Clara would like that," he said in what he hoped sounded like a regretful tone. "She's sort of the jealous type, if you know what I mean."

"Oh." Leslie's eyes rounded. "I got it. Not a problem. But, if things don't work out with Clara, we can have some fun together."

Dawson had absolutely no reply to that. He nodded and shut his door, sliding the lock into place so Leslie could hear it. He turned away from the door. Would Leslie say something to Clara about their conversation at the next yoga class? Would Clara be mad? He'd pretty much told Leslie that he and Clara were dating.

He crossed the room and picked up his cell phone. It was 10:00 on Sunday morning, and maybe Clara slept in longer. But this was sort of an emergency.

He pulled up her number and pressed CALL.

When she didn't answer, he debated about whether he should leave a message. "Hi, it's Dawson. Or Mr. Harris. Whichever you prefer. I might have just told Leslie a desperate lie. So I'm hoping that you'll call me back, soon, and I can explain."

He hung up and tried to return to reviewing the brief on his laptop, but he found himself checking his phone every few minutes. When it finally rang an hour later, he snatched it off the counter. Heart hammering, he answered, "You called back."

"Are you okay?" Clara asked, concern in her voice.

"I didn't mean to worry you," Dawson said quickly. "I just . . . uh . . . can you meet for lunch today?"

"Lunch?" Clara paused. "What's going on with Leslie?"

Dawson started pacing as he talked. His nerves were in a giant knot. He told her about the conversation at the door, and Clara started laughing.

"What's funny?" he asked.

"You opened the door without a shirt on?"

Dawson stopped pacing. "Is that a crime?"

"I saw how Leslie fawned all over you at the yoga class," Clara said. "You probably made one of her wildest dreams come true."

"I'm not interested in Leslie, and no matter how many times I turn her down, she doesn't get the message," Dawson said. "So I might have embellished a little about you and me."

"What do you mean?" Clara's tone instantly sounded wary.

Dawson explained how Leslie had invited him to lunch, and how he'd said he had lunch plans with Clara . . . then implied they were dating.

"We aren't dating," Clara said.

He tried not to let her bluntness sting. "I know," he said. "We're just hanging out, but I didn't think Leslie needed the clarification."

When Clara didn't say anything for a long time, Dawson looked at his phone to make sure they were still connected. "Clara?"

"Jeff told me your mom sometimes tries to set you up on dates," she finally said.

"Yes . . ."

"So that day you asked me to the symphony, you were looking to fill a ticket," she continued. "I'm thinking your mom was trying to set you up, and you were trying to get out of it."

"That's not exactly—"

"And now you're trying to get out of being pursued by Leslie by using me as an excuse."

Dawson exhaled. "I was going to call you anyway."

"Really?" Clara said, her tone doubtful. "You're a grown man, a successful attorney, and, well, I think you can tell Leslie the truth. Remember what we talked about at dinner the other night? How telling the truth from the very beginning can make our lives so much easier?"

"You're right," Dawson said. He didn't know whether to be impressed with Clara or to feel like he was a huge idiot—or maybe a combination of both. "You're absolutely right. Have you ever thought about going to law school?"

"No," she said with a laugh.

Dawson relaxed at the sound of her laugh. Maybe she wouldn't hang up on him after all.

"I'm an elementary school teacher," she said. "I was teaching kindergarten before I came to Pine Valley. You'd be surprised how much skill it takes to moderate the emotions and actions of five-year-olds."

He crossed to the couch in the living room and sat down. "What made you change your career?"

She seemed to hesitate for a moment. "My school was a private school, and it shut down temporarily because it was under investigation for financial fraud. About the same time things ended with my ex, and then my grandma had her stroke. After she died, I quit my job and decided to start over."

Dawson's mind reeled. "Wow. Any one of those things would have been tough, but all three?"

"What's the saying, 'When it rains it pours'?"

"Yeah, life can be strange that way," he said. "I'm sorry about your grandma and your job. Now that you told me, I can totally see you as a kindergarten teacher. I'll bet every five-year-old boy was in love with you."

Clara gave a soft laugh. "I might have gotten one or two love notes."

Dawson grinned. "I'd love to hear more about what brought you to Pine Valley, so I'm hoping that you'll want to get some lunch together."

"You're incorrigible."

"Is that a yes?" Dawson asked.

"Maybe."

"Ah, that word again." He groaned. "Okay, I'm going to Leslie's apartment right now, and I'm going to tell her the truth. Then around one o'clock I'll be standing in line at the Main Street Café, trying to decide if I want soup or a sandwich, or maybe both. I'll save you a seat in case you happen to show up. Deal?"

"I can see how you win court cases," Clara said.

Dawson heard the smile in her voice, and that was all he needed.

Five minutes later, he knocked on Leslie's apartment door. He'd never been to her apartment, but she'd told him which one it was plenty of times. Oh, and he'd also put on a shirt.

The door opened almost instantly, and Leslie's eyes about popped open when she saw him. That was truly a feat, because she'd certainly looked through her peephole before opening the door.

"Oh my gosh, you came!" Leslie stepped forward and threw her arms about his neck.

Dawson had no choice but to hug her back.

Leslie pulled back and grabbed his hand. "Come in. You're way early, but I can give you the grand tour."

Dawson disentangled his hand from hers. "I'm not coming for lunch," he said. "I just had to talk to you for a second. I sort of led you to believe that Clara and I were dating, and, well, we've been on one date. I don't know if we'll keep dating, but even if we don't, I don't want you to think that I'm going to eventually date you."

Leslie's eyes had gone from wide with surprise to narrow with confusion.

"You're a talented woman, Leslie, and you're fun to be around," Dawson continued, feeling like he'd just swallowed a mouthful of sand. "But I'm not attracted to you in a romantic sense. I wanted to be straight up with you so that I don't hurt your feelings, in case you have other expectations."

Leslie opened her mouth, then shut it. Then her face went a deep red. She stepped back, gripping the edge of her door so hard that her fingers turned white.

"I'm sorry," he said, trying to fill in the awkward silence. "I hope I didn't—"

With a sudden movement, Leslie swung the door toward him, and Dawson barely backed out of the way before it shut in his face.

He stood there for a moment, stunned. Obviously he'd embarrassed her, made her furious. Could he have worded things differently? Spoken less truth so she wouldn't be so mad? No, he told himself. It was better this way . . . at least he hoped. Leslie *was* a great person. She didn't deserve rejection. She also didn't deserve to be led on.

After another minute of staring at the door, and knowing that he'd said what needed to be said, he left Leslie's apartment. When he got back to his place, he sent Clara a text: *Just had a door slammed in my face. I guess there's a first time for everything.*

Clara replied right away: *Ouch. She doesn't want to be friends?*

I think her answer would be no, although I didn't dare knock again to find out.

Poor you. But you did the right thing, she wrote.

He hoped so. *If my apartment is on the news for being on fire, I have a lead on the arsonist.*

Ha. Ha. She'll get over you quicker than you think.

Not a compliment.

It's good for you to be taken down a notch once in a while.

Funny. I don't think I can take two rejections in one day. I'll be saving you a seat for lunch.

I hope you're crossing your fingers.

Dawson smiled and sent back the crossed-fingers emoji. He'd been teasing her, but he realized he was sort of serious as well. He felt pretty terrible about what had happened with Leslie, and spending time with Clara would make him feel better—especially since she'd been the one to tell him to confess the truth to Leslie.

Now that he thought about it more, it had been liberating. Yeah, it had been hard, uncomfortable, and awkward, but it had also been the right thing to do.

Nine

Clara paused before pulling the glass door open. Through the large windows she could see Dawson inside the Main Street Café. Of course, he was already sitting at a table, a drink in front of him, his fingers tapping away at his phone. He wasn't wearing a suit or tie, or even a dress shirt. In fact, he was wearing just a regular T-shirt.

Well, not even a T-shirt could look regular on Dawson Harris. No, it fit him in just the right way to show off his broad shoulders and sculpted arms without looking like he was trying to attract women like flies.

Clara reached for the door, because at any second he could look up, and she didn't want him to think she was spying on him . . . although she totally was. She didn't know what she liked better, that he'd dressed down or that he hadn't shaved. He was one of those guys who looked even better with some scruff. And for Dawson to look better was sort of amazing by itself.

She pulled the door open and stepped inside. The place was mostly empty, except for a young couple at the register ordering food.

Dawson looked up immediately, and a smile broke out on his face.

"Hi," she said, walking toward him. Her stomach felt all fluttery as his brown eyes surveyed her. Or maybe it was his smile. "Is this seat taken?"

"No," he said, standing up and pulling out the chair for her.

"I should order," she said.

"Have a seat, I'll order," he said. "What do you want?"

She'd been here enough times that she didn't need to look at the menu board. "I'll have the chicken salad sandwich on wheat."

"Anything to drink?"

"Lemonade," she said. "Thank you, sir."

He just winked and moved to the register. The couple who'd been there left and took one of the tables. Dawson ordered, then came back to the table.

"Did you already eat?" she asked, trying not to check out too much how great his jeans fit.

"I told them to hold my order until you arrived," he said, taking a seat across from her.

"What if I didn't arrive?"

"I'd be ravenous in about an hour."

Clara laughed. "I'm glad I'm not the reason for your hunger."

"I wouldn't exactly say that," Dawson said, picking up his phone. "Sorry, I need to finish this text. Then I want to hear all about your kindergarten students."

"All right," she said. "I don't know if my stories will be very entertaining though."

Dawson sent his text, then put his phone down. "I disagree. You said you received multiple love notes. Perhaps I can learn a thing or two from them."

"Maybe you can," Clara said. "I mean, it's hard to turn down a note that says, 'You're prettier than my mommy.'"

Dawson leaned back in his chair and laughed.

"My favorite one started out, 'My dad says you can live at my house.'"

"I hope you turned him down," Dawson said. "And I hope his mom didn't see the note."

"His parents were divorced, and I wouldn't be surprised if his dad had approved the note," Clara said. "He used to pick up his son and linger a little too long for my taste."

"I'm sure you had no problem turning him down and telling him exactly how you felt," Dawson said, his eyes gleaming.

"Not really."

They both laughed.

"So, tell me about Leslie," she said. "What did you say to make her slam the door on you?"

Dawson looked sheepish. He rubbed the back of his neck, glancing away for a moment. "I was honest, but maybe I was a little too blunt."

As he told her what he'd said, Clara decided he'd been kind, yet firm. "I think you did the right thing. It was up to Leslie how she wanted to react, and she was probably more embarrassed than anything. At least she knows where you stand."

"Yeah," Dawson said, his tone dull.

"Unless you *do* like her, and now you feel like you lost an opportunity."

He straightened, and his eyes flashed. "No, definitely not. Even if you weren't around, I'd still not be interested in Leslie."

"Good to know," Clara said.

He lifted his brows. "It's the truth."

Their sandwiches arrived, and Clara ignored the way Dawson's gaze had turned intense. She started to eat her sandwich, and he took the hint and began eating his food as well.

After a couple of minutes of eating, he said, "You know, my mom runs a book club, and they're always looking for new members."

"Really?" she said. "My grandma and I were in one for a few years until some of the women moved away."

"I don't know if they read romances, though," he said.

"I read all different types of books," Clara said. "Romances are my go-to when I want to relax and pretend like I don't have any problems."

"If that's how it's supposed to be, then maybe I need to rethink my strategy next time," he said.

"You mean not binge read all night?"

Dawson chuckled. "How did you know?"

"Um, because you read two books in less than a week," she said, "and I'm sure your work schedule didn't magically disappear."

"You're right." He reached for his drink and took a sip. "You're right about a lot of stuff. How do you do that?"

Clara smiled and gave a small shrug. "It's sort of how kindergarten teachers are. We just know stuff."

Dawson shook his head and laughed.

"Tell me what you thought about the books," Clara said. "Did you like one over the other?" She had to admit she was impressed when he seemed to be seriously thinking over her question.

"I think I learned that you can't lump all romances together," he said in a thoughtful tone. "They both had lots of feelings discussed, and of course there were the kissing scenes..."

Was he actually *blushing*?

He rubbed his neck. "I have to admit that I was interested to know how everything was going to play out. I mean, I knew they'd somehow get together in the end . . . but I got caught up in the story lines."

"That's nice to know you didn't consider them silly."

He lifted his brows.

"Oh . . . you did."

"Not silly as far as the stories and the writing," he said in a slow voice. "It was silly that I had to read them in order to see you again."

Clara smirked.

He leaned . . . He was making a habit of that. "Ironically, you making me read those books before I saw you again would be a good plot twist in a romance novel."

"Ha. Ha." She picked up her drink and took a sip. "Which book was your favorite?"

Again, he seemed to be thinking. "Nope. Can't choose. They were both decent reads. Although I found the Regency one intriguing because of all the social manners and expectations." He waved a hand toward her. "You and I meeting here would be considered scandalous. Even though we're in a public place, you should have a chaperone."

Clara laughed. "And you should still be married. Divorce wasn't allowed back then. Men just had mistresses."

Dawson didn't seem fazed at her comment. "It's remarkable how strict and proper they seemed to be, yet, they turned a blind eye to stuff we'd find immoral today—like men having mistresses when they were married."

"Irony at its best."

Dawson nodded, his gaze moving over her face.

Clara took another sip from her drink. She was going to be very hydrated by the end of their lunch.

"So are you looking to teach again?" he asked. "Or does Jeff Finch pay you too much?"

"He pays decent," Clara said. "Teaching school is a lot different, of course, and I had summers off. I'll miss that part, but I needed a break from teaching."

"Was your last class tough?" he asked.

"Kids see right through fake in an instant," she said. "It became harder and harder to show up to class when my entire life had shifted."

"You went through a lot, and it sounds like you had to deal with everything on your own."

Clara nodded. "I survived, and now I'm here. I'm glad Jeff took a chance on me and hired me."

"Me too." Dawson took another sip of his drink. He'd finished his sandwich already. "I hope things will be better in Pine Valley and that you'll be happy here."

The sincerity in his voice was genuine, and Clara felt her heart twinge. "Thanks, Dawson."

His eyes widened. "Did you call me *Dawson*?"

Clara smiled. "I did."

He stood and cleared off their wrappers from the table. "I think that calls for a celebration."

"What are you talking about?" Clara said with a laugh.

He held out his hand, and she put hers in his. She figured he was just being a gentleman and helping her up from the chair. But he kept ahold of it as he led her outside. She supposed she could have pulled away from his grasp, but she enjoyed the warm strength of it.

"Where are we going?" she asked as they started walking along the street, passing her car and his truck.

"Do you want to check out the bookstore?" he asked, looking down at her. "We could buy matching books for our celebration."

Clara was having a hard time focusing on anything other than his hand holding hers.

"My mom told me the book they're doing for book club," he continued, "and I thought maybe we could read it, too."

"Dawson, I don't think so," Clara said, coming to a stop. "I'm sure your mom is a great lady, but wouldn't it be sort of presumptuous of us? I mean, it's not like we're dating or anything."

Dawson looked pointedly at their linked fingers. "I'd like to be dating you."

She looked down at their linked fingers, and slowly she pulled her hand away.

"You did call me Dawson," he said with an unrepentant grin.

"True," she said. "I'm not really into PDA, even if you were my boyfriend."

"Well," Dawson said, leaning down so that his mouth was close to her ear. "If I were your boyfriend, I'd work really hard to change your mind."

Warm tingles rushed through Clara at his nearness. His clean, spicy scent was just as she remembered from the other night. It had been rather nice to hold his hand, but she felt like it was giving him too much of an expectation. Regardless, she hoped he couldn't hear the thudding of her heart. "Current Clara knows that Future Clara won't agree."

Dawson drew away with a chuckle. They started walking in the direction of the bookstore again.

"Despite the fact that you're not taking me seriously," she said, "I think we can be friends."

"I'm totally taking you seriously," he said, raising his hands. "See? No PDA? I'm just wondering how your ex put up with all your rules."

This thought sobered Clara. "Good question," she said. "Maybe it was his rule, not mine."

They'd reached the bookstore, and Dawson paused before opening the door. "Well, if it was his rule, and not yours, that makes me feel a lot better." He pulled the door open, and Clara passed by him to enter the bookstore.

She wasn't sure how she'd been talked into coming to the bookstore with Dawson. All she knew was that she had to guard her heart. When she gave Dawson an inch, he was more than happy to take two.

Clara paused by the front display table of new releases while Dawson walked to the rack of magazines. He picked up a *Fish & Game* magazine. Clara watched him flip through the pages; then she turned back to her own browsing. Only one employee and another customer were in the store. Clara picked up a book and read the back cover, but then realized she hadn't internalized a thing. It was hard to focus when Dawson was standing only a few feet away.

She had to admit to herself that she liked him, really liked him. Despite their differences.

When another several minutes passed, and when it seemed that Dawson was actually reading an article from the magazine, Clara left her place and joined him at the magazine rack. "So, what's the book club book you were telling me about?"

He looked up, seeming surprised at the question, when in fact, she knew he wasn't.

"Hang on, let me see what my mom texted over." He set the magazine on the shelf in front of him and pulled out his cell from his pocket.

Clara watched his actions and tried to ignore how her stomach had just flipped over.

"She said . . ." He scrolled through messages on his phone. "*My Lady Jane.* That's a weird title. Is it another Regency?"

Clara pulled out her own phone and looked up the book on Amazon. She read through the book description. "It's a historical novel—a parody, it looks like, with some fantasy thrown in."

"Fantasy? Like *Lord of the Rings*?"

"Yeah, that's fantasy," she said. "It might be interesting." She clicked the *Buy Now* button. "Got it."

"Wait, what?" Dawson said, leaning over to look at her phone. "You bought it online?"

"Yeah, the Kindle version."

He blinked his eyes, and he was so close, she could feel his warm breath tickle her neck. "I thought we were going to buy books together."

"You can still buy the paperback," Clara said. "Do you want me to see if they have it in the store?"

Dawson frowned. "Maybe I'll just get the Kindle version too. Do I have to get a Kindle to read it?"

Clara moved back slightly and leaned against the magazine rack. Dawson was simply too close for her to hold a decent conversation. "You can download the Kindle app on your phone."

He exhaled. "I think I'd prefer the paperback form. Or is it in hardcover?"

"Let's ask and find out."

But Dawson didn't move, which pretty much meant that Clara was trapped, unless she wanted to brush past him. He had that intense look in his eyes again.

"What?" she prompted.

"I was just wondering what other rules your ex had."

Ten

Dawson was starting to become familiar enough with Clara's various expressions that he could tell if he was going to get a brush-off from her or an actual answer. When she'd told him that she didn't like PDA, he'd taken it in stride. Some people didn't. As for him, he'd had no problem with it. Early in his relationship with Romy, they'd been plenty affectionate in public. But as their marriage wore on, they seemed to see each other less and less, so the opportunities had been few.

Clara saying that her ex had "rules" was hard to ignore, and his curiosity had only been growing by the minute. Was her ex some sort of control freak? If so, then he was glad their relationship had ended. Whether anything worked out between him and Clara, she didn't deserve that sort of relationship. Besides, she was too smart to get involved with someone like that, right? Although, he'd heard of stories of men dating toxic women, and vice versa.

Right now, she was staring at him like *he* was crazy, and he knew he wasn't going to get an answer to his question. Although he didn't mind her staring at him; he could get used to that pretty quickly.

"It's probably not fair to compare my ex to another guy," she said at last. "Everyone's different, that's all."

He tried to hold back a smile. "So you keep telling me." He wanted to reach for her hand again but decided he'd better wait for her to make the next move. She seemed interested, and they'd had some good conversations amid all the bantering, so that gave him some hope. Hope for what, he wasn't sure. The long list of failures Romy had written up came to mind, and he hadn't conquered any of them. Why would he want to put those faults onto another woman?

"Where did you go?" Clara said, touching his arm. Her fingers were warm, soft, and he wondered if this gesture could be considered the "next move."

Dawson blinked. "What do you mean?"

Her fingers moved down his arm, then dropped away. "You just sort of looked like you'd left the country or something."

"Oh," he said, lifting his hand and rubbing the back of his neck. "With all this talk of exes, I was reminded of my list of failures."

Clara's brows drew together.

"You know, when your ex writes up all the things she hates about you."

"Um . . . I don't know," she said. "That sounds pretty brutal. I hope you burned the list."

What was it about Clara's blue eyes? They were so steady and unwavering. "Nope. It's in a file somewhere."

Clara shook her head. "She really wrote a list?"

"It was more like a series of paragraphs, three pages to be exact," Dawson said.

"Can I help you find something?" a woman's voice cut in.

Dawson looked over to see the bookstore employee approaching them. It was the same brunette who'd helped him before—Felicity. The other customer in the store seemed to have left. He was about to say no thanks, then thought better of it. "Do you have the book called *My Lady Jane,* by, um—"

"Oh, the one with the three authors," Felicity said. "Brodi Ashton is one of them. I'll check. That one has been popular."

While Felicity left them alone again to walk to the register at the sales counter, Clara picked up the *Fish & Game* magazine he'd set down. "I'll buy this for you, my treat."

When he started to protest, she put her hand on his chest. "You paid for dinner last week, and lunch today. It's my turn. Besides, I think a good fishing story is the perfect antidote against letters from ex-wives."

Normally, Dawson wouldn't have agreed. Nothing was an antidote against his list of failures. But how could he argue with Clara's hand on his chest? He put his hand over hers and squeezed.

"Okay," he said.

"Okay." She laughed and pulled her hand out of his grasp, then walked to the register, magazine in hand.

He watched her for a moment, then followed her.

Felicity had found a copy of *My Lady Jane*. When she looked up, she said, "Weren't you the guy in here the other day buying a couple of romances?"

Dawson squared his shoulders. "Yep. That was me. I enjoyed both of them."

Even though he wasn't looking at Clara, he could practically see her holding back a laugh.

Felicity didn't even crack a smile. "Great to hear. You'll enjoy this one too, especially if you like horses."

Clara looked over at Dawson with anticipation, but he couldn't meet her gaze, because then he'd start laughing.

"It will be $21.55 for both," Felicity said with a nod.

Clara plunked a debit card on the counter and gave him a don't-argue-with-me look. He stepped back and let her complete the transaction. When Felicity handed over the sack with both items inside, Clara passed it off to Dawson.

"Thank you," he said, feeling like a kid thanking his mom for ice cream. Although Clara was nothing like his mom.

They left the shop together, with Dawson thinking fast about how else he could prolong this afternoon with Clara. He had plenty of work to do, but he was reluctant to say goodbye to Clara.

His phone buzzed, and he looked at the incoming call. His mom was calling; it was like she knew he'd just thought of her.

"Uh oh," he said, slipping his phone back into his pocket after selecting the "Can I call you later" option. They were almost to his truck, and Clara's car was only a couple of spots away.

"What is it?" she asked.

"My mom," he said, slowing his step. "She's onto me."

Clara slowed with him and gave him a quizzical look.

"I sent her a text asking her when the next book club is," he said, "and told her I might have a friend who's interested."

"You can call her if you need to," Clara said. "I've got to get home and get my Sunday afternoon nap in. It's one of my rules. You know, Sunday naps."

He lifted his brows.

She shook her head.

He stared at her, and she stared back, one side of her mouth lifted in a smirk. Too bad she hated PDA, or he might be tempted to kiss her right in the middle of the sidewalk. Still, he leaned in, just a little, to see what she would do.

She stepped away. "Enjoy your magazine," she said, moving farther and farther from him.

"Wait," he said. "When are we going to read the book?" He held up the sack.

"I might start tonight," she said, lifting her brows as if she were challenging him.

"Me too," he said. He'd slept longer than usual, which meant he'd probably be up later too.

"Sounds like a plan," she said. "Have a good rest of the day."

Dawson lifted his hand in a half-hearted wave. By the time he reached the driver's side of his truck and climbed in, she'd already driven away. He leaned his head back and closed his eyes for a second. Yep, he could still see that sassy smile of hers in his mind.

He secured his Bluetooth and called his mom.

"Hello, son," she said as soon as she answered. "Who is this woman?"

"What are you talking about?" he said, pulling onto Main Street.

"I just ran into Jeff Finch, and we got talking," his mom said. "Then I put two and two together about your questions on book club."

Dawson stifled his groan. If he was unequivocally dating Clara, then he'd be fine with this conversation. But so far, everything he'd suggested about his parents had been shut down. First, the symphony, then the book club suggestion. Although that still had potential.

"Her name is Clara Benson, and we're friends."

"Uh-huh," she said, sounding doubtful. "Does this have anything to do with the real reason you turned down the symphony tickets and refused to come to the luncheon that included Paula Smith?"

"Paula Smith doesn't factor into this," Dawson said, slowing his truck and stopping at the light. "I'm not going to date Paula, period."

"Tell me about this Clara woman."

His mom didn't mince words, which sort of reminded him of Clara, when he thought about it.

"She's a kindergarten teacher," he said. "She moved to Pine Valley a few months ago to start over after her grandma died."

"That is quite the change," his mom said. "Jeff says she's a redhead."

Dawson wanted to laugh. Where was his mom going with this? "I don't see Jeff telling you that, unless you asked him what she looked like."

"Hmm," his mom said, and Dawson could just picture her pursing her mouth, creating those little vertical lines. "You're a tall man, and I just don't picture you with a short redhead. You know that redheads have personalities that can be demanding? Especially the women."

Dawson was trying really hard to not let his mom's words get under his skin. She was tall, willowy, and blonde—which now came from a bottle to cover up any grays. "If you ask me, it's refreshing to date a woman who isn't afraid to speak her mind. It really takes the guess work out of things, and I'm not anticipating a three-page letter any time soon that picks apart every single one of my flaws."

His mom went silent. Dawson hadn't meant to take such

a deep jab, at her and himself. In Romy's letter, she'd included several things she'd been upset with about his parents.

"Well, you know me," his mom said at last, her tone softer now. "Don't judge someone until you get to know them. But I thought you said you weren't dating."

He exhaled. "We've hung out a couple of times." Like five minutes ago. "She was recently in a serious relationship, and well, you know my history, so she wants to keep things casual for now."

"And you?" his mom prompted.

Dawson paused. "I agree we should take things slow, but I like her. Believe me, I'm as surprised as anyone would be. And it has nothing to do with the color of her hair."

His mom clicked her tongue.

"I don't know where any of this is going," he continued. "But if you meet her, I expect you and Dad to be on your best behavior."

"Oh, Dawson," his mom chided, but there was humor in her tone. "You won't have to worry about me. I'm always polite to your dates."

"Agreed, but you could also be *friendly*?" Dawson had arrived at his condo parking lot. He pulled into his assigned space and shut off the ignition. "Clara's bright, intelligent, and she's been through a lot of hard things, so I'm not really ready to hear someone criticize her."

"I wasn't—okay, I'm just curious, that's all." His mom sighed. "You went through the wringer with Romy, and no one would blame me for watching out for my son."

It was Dawson's turn to sigh. "I'm fine, Mom. You're the one who's been trying to set me up. Clara is the first woman I've even been interested in since my divorce. And don't worry, I'm quite enjoying being friends with her."

His mom cleared her throat. "All right then, dear. I look forward to meeting Clara sometime."

She couldn't be making it more obvious that she didn't exactly approve, and she wanted to meet Clara in order to put in her two cents. Dawson had no doubt that Clara could hold her own around his mom, but he didn't want his mom to get the idea that she could in any way influence his love life.

Love life. Dawson hadn't thought of himself in that context for a long time... maybe ever.

After hanging up with his mom, he climbed out of his truck and snatched the sack from the bookstore. He smiled to himself as he thought about how Clara had bought the book and magazine for him. She was definitely not a pushover or looking to be treated like a princess.

It was a different experience walking to his front door and not seeing any sign of Leslie lurking around corners. He entered his apartment, set the sack on the counter, and powered on his laptop. While he was out, Mandy, his paralegal, had emailed back the final formatted brief. It should only take a few minutes to double-check a few things, then on to the next case he had to review. Mandy had researched the details of both sides of the case and sent over her summary and links to more information. He had to go through it all before his Monday morning appointment with a new client who'd been sued by her former brother-in-law for her dead husband's portion of the family business.

An hour later, he realized he wasn't as focused on reviewing Mandy's research as he should have been.

He kept thinking about his mom's assumptions about Clara, and he realized they only made him want to spend more time with her. He wondered if it was too soon to text her. He eyed the sack from the bookstore, then took out *My Lady Jane*.

He'd read a chapter or two, then text Clara to see if she'd started.

Dawson settled on his couch and opened the book. He wasn't an expert on British history, but the authors made it clear that the story was based on a fractured re-telling, with, people who shape-shifted into various animals. It was all rather ridiculous, but Dawson found himself laughing aloud in the first chapter.

He reached for his phone and texted Clara. *This book is hilarious.*

Her reply came a few minutes later. *You already started? I'm impressed.*

I have to get back to my legal research for a case soon, but I'm finding Edward a misguided, yet compelling character.

Wow, you should be in a book club. Misguided, yet compelling?

Dawson typed back a face-wink emoji.

Clara was too smart, as usual. *Ok. Nice distraction. What did your mom say?*

Dawson abandoned the texting and called her.

She answered on the first ring. "That bad, huh?"

"Nothing bad," Dawson countered. "My mom would have figured things out eventually, but she ran into Jeff Finch today."

"Uh oh."

"It's all good," Dawson said. "Don't worry. I told my mom we're just friends."

Eleven

The irony in Dawson's voice was plain, and Clara smiled to herself. "How did your mom react to that?"

"Oh, she didn't buy it for a minute," he said. "She wants to meet you, of course."

"She sounds like a very *interested* mother." His mom sounded pushy, if Clara was going to tell the truth. She'd been doing the dishes when Dawson had started texting her, so now that he called, she moved through her small apartment and sat on the cheap couch that had come with the "fully furnished" apartment.

"Normally, she wouldn't be like this," he continued, "but the divorce put my parents on edge. Now that some time has passed, my mom thinks she can set me up with just the right woman."

Definitely a pushy mother. "Anyone in particular?"

"Her most recent effort was actually a girl I used to date in high school," Dawson said. "She's divorced with two little kids now."

Well, it sounded like his mom was pretty open-minded if she was trying to set her son up with a single mom. Clara leaned back against the couch. "Instant parenthood?"

"Yep," Dawson said with a chuckle. "That doesn't bother me as much as my old girlfriend. There's a reason we broke up."

"Oh, do tell," Clara said. "I love high school drama."

Dawson laughed. "I guess I was the only who thought we were exclusive, because I found out Paula had two other guys dangling from her fingertips."

"Ouch," Clara said. "That's probably worse in high school when guys and girls get so infatuated with each other. Maybe Paula would like my ex. He's into the whole multiple-relationships thing."

"He cheated on you?"

Clara swallowed. Maybe she'd let on too much. "It was more than cheating," she said. "His affair had gone on more than a year."

Dawson was quiet for a moment. "I'm sorry."

"I used to be sorry, but not anymore," she said. "When my grandma died, I was able to make a clean break from everything. If I hadn't found out when I did about Max, I probably would have kept living his lies."

"Truth is always better," he said in a quiet voice.

"Yes, even when it's painful."

"Truth—did you have fun today?" Dawson asked.

"With you?" Clara teased. It was nice to have the conversation become more lighthearted.

"Yes, with me."

A warm shiver traveled through her body, and she pulled her legs up onto the couch. "I did. Thank you for inviting me."

She could hear the smile in his voice when he next spoke. "It was my pleasure."

"Truth?"

"Absolutely," Dawson said, his voice warm. "I'm thinking we should go to dinner on, say, Tuesday? We have a book to discuss."

Clara shook her head and laughed. "You're extremely persistent."

"And convincing?"

"That too," she said. "Since it looks like I might be changing my yoga class schedule, Tuesday might actually work."

"I hope Leslie isn't weird around you," Dawson said.

"I'm already going to a different class." Clara leaned forward. Talking to Dawson on the phone was making her want to see him again. "We can text on Tuesday to see if it still works for both of us."

"Do I have to wait until Tuesday to text you?" Dawson teased.

"You know," Clara started, "when I said I was fine with being friends, I didn't mean *best* friends."

Dawson laughed. "Friends or best friends, I'll take it."

Clara grinned.

"I hate to do this," he said. "Especially since I'm the one who called you. But it looks like Mandy has sent me about three emails since we've been on the phone."

"Mandy?"

"My paralegal," he said. "We have a new case we're starting tomorrow, so this weekend has been about doing our due diligence."

"Ah, so you're not the only workaholic?" Clara said.

"No, and believe me, I'm working on my nasty habits. Today, in fact, was a banner day. Going to lunch and hanging out with you—well, let's just say that you've been good for me, Miss Benson."

The sincerity of his tone reached deep into Clara's heart. "Glad I could help, friend."

His chuckle was soft.

"I'll let you go, then," she continued. "As for me, since I'm not preparing school lessons for this week, I'm off to read more, and maybe take a bath."

"Uh, you probably shouldn't say something like that to me."

Clara's body heated when she realized what he was referring to. She gave a weak laugh. After they hung up, she released a groan. Dawson was . . . overwhelming. Just as she'd told him that time in the office. Yet, she was already looking forward to Tuesday night. She wondered what else his mom had said about her. Clara sensed that Dawson was holding back on something. But there was no reason to push him on the topic, because Clara didn't have any plans to meet his mom. That would mean they'd be officially dating.

The thought only made Clara feel fluttery inside, and that probably wasn't a good thing. It was becoming harder and harder to keep her distance from Dawson.

She didn't hear from him for an entire two hours, and when a text came through from Dawson, she laughed.

Want to move the dinner to Monday night instead?

She wrote back: *Maybe.*

He texted back a broken-hearted emoji.

Tuesday or Monday, whichever night they had dinner, seemed too long to wait.

But Clara didn't see him until Wednesday. Monday, he texted and proposed Tuesday again. Then Tuesday he texted an apology and said he'd call her later that night. Clara fell asleep before he called, and on Wednesday morning she found that he'd called about 11:30 p.m. He hadn't left a message, but he'd sent a text that said: *Wednesday, promise.*

She hadn't expected him to appear at her office, though. Jeff was out showing houses to a client, and 4:00 p.m. was proving to be the dead hour as usual. She just happened to be gazing out the window, possibly thinking of Dawson, and if he'd actually follow through, when she saw his red truck pull up in front of the office and come to a stop.

She smoothed her hair and wondered if her makeup was mostly worn off. The day was warm, so she'd worn a linen blouse, yellow skirt, and heeled sandals. She wouldn't feel so short next to Dawson. She rose from her desk as he opened the front door and came into the office.

He wore a dark-gray suit, and she knew from their previous texts that he'd had court appearances that day.

"Hi," Dawson said, sounding like he was out of breath.

"If you're looking for Jeff, he's not here," Clara teased, coming around the desk.

Dawson's gaze moved over her as he walked toward her.

"How did court go today?" she asked.

But instead of answering, he stepped closer and wrapped his arms around her, pulling her into a hug.

"Oh." This she hadn't expected. And she wondered if he was okay. She hugged him back, mostly on instinct, but had to admit that it felt great. *He* felt great. Not that she'd doubted, but her imaginings hadn't led her astray. And she probably shouldn't let herself breathe in his spicy scent. She knew it would be hard to let him go.

"Sorry about the PDA," he said against her ear, but he didn't let her go. "I just missed you."

Clara tried to ignore the *missed-you* comment; she'd

missed him too, which told her she was entering the danger zone. "Good thing no one's in the office, then."

Dawson drew away and released her. "It's okay for friends to hug, right?"

He was smiling, and this made her feel better. He wasn't hugging her because something terrible had happened and he was looking for comfort. He was hugging her because he missed her.

She nodded and rested a hand on the desk next to her, looking for a little more stability. Dawson's arms around her had given her a heady feeling.

"So, I called your boss," Dawson continued. "And I asked him if I could steal you early from work."

Clara stared at him. "You called Jeff?"

"Yeah." He had the decency to look a little sheepish. "I thought that, you know, we could get a head start on our evening if you could get out of the office sooner."

She opened her mouth, then shut it. Dawson could be both sweet and infuriating at the same time.

"Was ... that okay?"

She placed a hand on her hip. "Don't go over my head next time."

His mouth twitched.

"I mean it." She tried to sound firm, but she was failing at it.

He raised both of his hands. "I promise I won't go over your head again. I sort of had a plan in mind, and I had to call Jeff about something else anyway."

Clara exhaled. "What plan?"

"There's a great seafood place I want to take you to, but it's about an hour drive."

Dawson looked so earnest, and so hopeful, that Clara

couldn't help but smile. "You can spare that much time away from work?" she asked.

"I know, it's a miracle," he said. "But I was starting to go crazy without seeing you for so long."

Clara raised her brows.

"Too much truth?" he asked, moving closer again.

He grasped her hand, and Clara felt like her heart was about to leap out of her chest. "Um," she said, placing her other hand on his chest to stop him from leaning closer. Because if she wasn't careful, she might just allow him to keep leaning until they were kissing. He was warm, solid, and she shouldn't be touching him again, especially so soon after his hug. "I'll grab my purse. You can bring me back to my car later." She stepped away, pulling away from his hand, and his touch, and his scent.

She had to clear her head, which might be difficult if they were going to be together for the next few hours. She felt Dawson's gaze on her as she walked around the desk and picked up her purse. Then she powered down the office computer and switched on the answering service.

Straightening, she said, "Ready?" There was no time to check her appearance or freshen up.

"Great," he said, his mouth lifting into a half smile. They walked out of the front entrance, and Clara flipped off the lights and locked the door.

Dawson opened the passenger door for her, and she climbed into the truck. It was warm inside from the sun, and she was starting to feel at home in his truck.

He jumped in, started the truck, then pulled out his phone. "I told Mandy I'd be out of reach the rest of the day." He turned the phone off and set it on top of the console.

"Can you do that?" Clara asked. "I mean, the world might end."

"Well, if it does, we can fight zombies together."

Clara smirked. "Sounds good." Just then her phone buzzed, and she looked down at it. "What did you tell Jeff?"

Dawson glanced over, his brow arched. "Why?"

"I think you know why," she said, turning her phone toward him. "Jeff just texted me: *Have a nice time, but don't let Dawson boss you around. Make him treat you right.*"

"I didn't tell him much."

Clara narrowed her eyes.

"Okay, I might have said that your ex-boyfriend was a jerk," he said in a slow voice, "and that he had a bunch of rules."

"I never said that."

"Uh, you sort of did."

Clara exhaled. She wrote Jeff back: *Don't worry. And thanks.*

She put her phone into her purse and said, "All right. Max sort of did have rules, but doesn't everyone? At least preferences. I was willing to do things his way, I guess."

Dawson slowed for a traffic light. "I'm surprised at that. I mean, you barely give me an inch."

"Yeah, well, I learned my lesson," Clara said. "When I found out that Max had been cheating on me almost our whole relationship, I decided that the next guy I dated wouldn't be making all the decisions."

"That's how it should be anyway," he said. "Wait. Am I the next guy you're dating?"

Clara cracked a smile. "That's not what I said."

"You also didn't tell me what Max's rules were." He raised his brows at her, then looked back at the road and merged onto the highway.

"He told me he hated PDA, but I wonder if that was just because he was in love with another woman and didn't want someone she knew to see us," Clara said in a thoughtful tone. "He never wanted to hang out two nights in a row . . . which should have been another clue. We'd hang out at my house and I'd cook dinner. Never going to his apartment should have been another clue. I was really dense, wasn't I?"

"Wait—you cook?" Dawson asked.

"You would pick up on that," she said with a laugh. "I can make the basics, nothing fancy."

"I'm sure it's better than my bachelor fare of heated soup and frozen dinners."

"You look more like a guy who drinks protein shakes," Clara said.

"Oh, I'm a whiz with the blender, but I don't consider that cooking." He looked over at her. "Really, what kinds of things do you cook?"

Clara shook her head. "Why are you so interested?"

He shrugged. "My mom didn't cook, so about the only homemade food I had growing up was pancakes on the weekends that my dad fixed."

"Poor kid," Clara said. "Your mom didn't bake you cookies after school?"

"Do you bake cookies?" Dawson was quick to ask.

"Not when there's just one of me."

Dawson exhaled. "At least you didn't say *maybe*."

Clara grinned. "I'm just going to keep you in suspense, and then maybe I'll cook for you one day and surprise you."

"I think that's the best thing I've heard in my entire life."

Twelve

Dawson wondered how soon was too soon to kiss Clara. Would tonight be pushing it? Would she be annoyed? Would she call off their "friendship"? Because he was thinking of her a lot more deeply than he ever had any *friend*.

She seemed to be enjoying the restaurant, so he was glad he'd suggested it. He'd only been a little antsy about not having his phone on, but it wasn't half as bad as he'd thought it would be. In fact, it was rather freeing. One of the items on the list of failures Romy had written up was that he never turned his phone off.

Yes, her list had hurt, but she had also been right about several things. He was a slave to his phone, and he'd always come up with every justification possible. And even though he knew he had to make changes, and was working on several things, he also knew that if he'd made these changes during his marriage, it still wouldn't have helped. Romy had completely distanced herself from him and disengaged. If she'd wanted him to change, hoped that he would change for her, then she would have suggested counseling instead of filing for divorce.

No, she hadn't wanted him—as his flawed self or as his changed self.

Deep down, he knew that if he were to have a successful relationship with another woman, he'd have to swallow his pride and start making those changes. It wasn't realistic for him to turn off his phone every night, but he could find times to do it. Such as this date with Clara.

"Dessert?" he asked Clara.

She shook her head with a groan. They'd shared the seafood platter, and in addition to the warm, crusty bread the restaurant was famous for. Dawson was full too. "We could split something."

"I'm going to have to take up running if I keep this up," Clara said. "Yoga won't combat all of the calories I ate tonight."

"You shouldn't worry," Dawson said. It bothered him when women put themselves down for their weight, but at least Clara ate like a normal person. Still . . . "You're pretty much perfect."

"Pretty much?" Clara said. "That means there's still something you think I can work on?"

The way she analyzed every bit of their conversation was one thing Dawson liked about her. One of many things. She was never boring to talk to. "Everyone has flaws," he said.

Her brows shot up, and he laughed.

"Okay, Mr. Harris," she said. "What's one of my flaws? And you'd better tell the truth."

Truth. Another item on his list of failures. Romy had said he wasn't truthful after her miscarriage because he'd told her he would have married her even if she hadn't been pregnant. He just wouldn't have married her so soon. Unless more time together ended up driving them apart.

Right now, Clara was waiting for his answer. "You won't order dessert with me," he said. "That's a flaw."

"It would only be a flaw if I never ordered dessert, but I happen to be full, so it's not a flaw." She shrugged. "It's a wise choice for tonight."

The waiter came over, ready to take their dessert order. Dawson waited for Clara to turn down the waiter, but instead, she said, "We'll split the raspberry cheesecake. Can you bring two forks?" Her blue eyes sparkled at Dawson.

"One flaw erased," she said when the waiter left. "Any other flaws you want to hit me with?"

"I don't think you're ready to hear about any more," Dawson said. "They're pretty intense."

"I can take it," she said, her mouth turning up at the corners, her gaze expectant.

So Dawson took the plunge. "You haven't kissed me yet."

Clara laughed, and her cheeks turned pink. "I should have expected that. Also, I don't think that's a flaw. It's a wise decision."

"That's debatable."

"No, it's not," Clara said, still smiling.

This only gave Dawson hope, and he hoped he wasn't completely misreading Clara. Even though she held back a lot, he was pretty sure she was as interested in him as he was in her.

The waiter brought the cheesecake, and Clara dutifully ate a couple of bites, but then turned the remainder of the dessert over to him.

He finished the cheesecake off and then insisted on paying the bill.

"You drove here, using your gasoline," Clara protested.

"That's okay," he said. "You can pay next time, and I'll order my own dessert."

Clara started to thaw. "All right, but I'm not going to let you forget."

Dawson rose from the table and extended his hand toward Clara. "How could I forget—you just said you'd go out with me again."

She put her hand in his, and he loved the way their fingers fit together. And she didn't pull her hand away once she stood, so he kept a hold of it as they walked out of the restaurant.

Night had fallen, and the warm spring air had grown cool.

When Clara shivered, he said, "Cold?"

"A little," she said.

He was only being a gentleman when he draped his arm around her shoulders.

"You're pushing it, Mr. Harris," she said, but there was a softness in her voice.

Squeezing her shoulder, he said, "Just let me know when you want to correct your flaw of not kissing me."

They slowed as they reached the passenger side of the truck, and Clara turned to look up at him.

Dawson's pulse jumped—maybe *she* would kiss *him*.

"You know, Mr. Harris, you're a charming guy," she said, reaching up and placing her hand over his heart. "But remember, we're just friends."

Then, she lifted up on her toes and kissed his cheek.

He wanted to pull her against him, press his mouth against hers and claim a real kiss. But she'd already drawn away and was waiting for him to open the door, a mischievous smile on her face.

"I know we're friends," he said. "But that was *not* the kind of kiss I was talking about."

She folded her arms and tilted her head, waiting for him to open the door. He sighed and unlocked the door. After she climbed in, he shut the door and walked around the front of the truck to the other side. He was both hopeful and impatient at the same time, and he wasn't sure how to explain that mixture of feelings.

He'd just spent the first evening he could remember in a long time without thinking about his work to-do list. He'd been so focused on Clara that he'd almost forgotten all the things he had to get done before another court date tomorrow. Spending these few hours with Clara would mean that he might be pulling an all-nighter. But at this point he didn't care. It would be worth it.

When he climbed in and started the truck, he said, "So, tell me about all this cooking you and your grandma used to do."

Clara laughed. "You're really hung up on that, aren't you?"

Dawson grinned. "I guess I am. I'm not even hungry, but I can't help but wonder what you might cook for me."

She shook her head. "You act as if you've never had a woman cook for you. I mean, didn't your wife cook?" She covered her mouth. "Sorry, I didn't mean to imply—"

"It's okay," he said as he pulled onto the highway heading back to Pine Valley. "Romy didn't cook; she was like my mom there. So it never really bothered me. I'd make dinner a couple of nights a week—but it was really just breakfast food. Omelets, pancakes, waffles. Unless we had a double date with another couple, or ate someplace with my parents, we were pretty much on our own, since our schedules didn't match up."

"Where did she work?" Clara asked.

"She worked as a dental hygienist for a couple of years. Then she went part time and started working at a gym too," he said. "It was probably the only fight we ever had ... if you don't count serving me divorce papers."

"Sorry," she said.

Dawson shrugged. "It feels like a long time ago now. If we could ever spend time together, it would be weekends. But she was at the gym during the times that I was home. I guess I should have seen that as a major red flag. She told me she was trying to pay off my law school loans faster, but during the divorce proceedings, I found that she'd never paid anything extra toward the school loans. I was paying the minimum, of course. And it wasn't like I expected her to pay for my loans—but that had been her justification to work at the gym on weekends."

"When *did* you see each other?" Clara asked, sounding genuinely curious.

"Mornings," Dawson said. "At least, I saw her sleeping in our second bedroom before I left for work in the mornings." He paused. He hadn't meant to get that personal.

Clara was quiet for a moment.

"She said I snored," he said at last. "I believed her, completely ignoring the fact that we had no sex life at that point anyway." He'd already confessed that his wife slept in their guest room, so why not more? "But last year, I went to a legal convention, and I ended up sharing a room with another guy in my firm. I warned him that I snored, and I'd help pay for an extra room if he needed it. But, over the course of three nights, he said he never heard me snore."

Clara exhaled. "First, there are lots of remedies for snoring, and second, I'm sorry Romy wasn't honest with you."

He felt her gaze on him, and the compassion in her voice made him feel that maybe he hadn't been such a big jerk in his marriage after all.

Clara rested her hand over his. "Even if there were problems in your marriage, if your wife wouldn't talk to you about them, then how could you fix anything?"

Dawson turned his hand palm up, linked their fingers. Just holding Clara's hand made his heart race, especially since she'd initiated the contact.

"She didn't want to fix anything," he said. "And I was so caught up in my new job that I ignored the signs."

"Hey," Clara said, squeezing his hand lightly. "You're talking to a woman who was engaged to a man who was in another long-term relationship. At least Romy wasn't cheating on you, because being blind to that makes me a first-class dunce."

Dawson sped up the truck to get around a slower car. He'd tightened his grip on Clara's hand without realizing it.

"Dawson, are you okay?" she asked.

He loosened his grip and slowed his speed. "I don't know if she was cheating on me. I look back now, and there were signs—signs I'd ignored, of course."

"Oh," Clara said in a faint voice.

"She never came home from the gym until close to midnight. I assumed it closed at 11:00 p.m., but after our divorce I found out it closed at 10:00 p.m. Even finding that out, I continued to justify that she might be cleaning workout equipment or something."

"Did you ever ask her?" she asked.

"I don't think I wanted to know," he said, glancing over

at her to find that she was gazing at him. "I mean, it would only add insult to injury."

Clara bit her lip. "The more I learn about Romy, the less I like her. I mean, I know she wrote you a letter with all of her complaints, but I'm thinking you could write a similar letter to her."

Dawson raised his brows. "You know, I think you're right." He tugged her hand toward him and kissed her knuckles. She didn't pull away. "But I think I'd like to keep Romy in the past."

"Sounds like a plan," Clara said in a soft voice.

Then she leaned her head against his shoulder, and Dawson felt like he'd won the lottery.

Thirteen

The hum of Dawson's truck and the warmth of his solid shoulder beneath her head made Clara doze off. She awoke when he pulled up to the curb in front of the realty office on Main. She felt like she was in a bit of a haze, and it took her a moment to grasp the reality that she'd fallen asleep on Dawson's shoulder.

"We're here," he said in a quiet voice as she lifted her head.

It was then that she realized she'd looped her left arm around his right. And it was deliciously comfortable. And now that she was aware of it, her pulse started to race. She drew away from him and used her hand to stifle a yawn. "I can't believe I fell asleep." She blinked in the dimness.

"Maybe I was boring you," Dawson teased in his low voice.

Clara scoffed. "No. Your truck was just warm and comfortable, I guess, and I did eat a lot." She neglected to tell him that *he* was warm and comfortable. She hadn't fallen asleep in a car or any vehicle since she was a kid.

He shut off the engine of his truck. "Is Jeff working you all hours?"

"Not really," Clara said. "We're busy, but it's a good busy. I've had a hard time sleeping through the night since—well, since everything fell apart back home."

Dawson's eyes met hers, and even though the only light inside the truck was coming from a streetlamp, she could feel the intensity of his gaze. "That gives us something else in common."

"Oh really?"

"Yeah, Mr. Insomniac here."

Clara grimaced. "Sorry, it's awful. I know."

"Maybe next time I'm awake at 3:00 a.m. with no hope of falling back asleep, I'll text you."

Clara shrugged as if it wouldn't be a big deal for him to call her in the middle of the night, but she was sort of thinking it crossed the boundaries of a casual friendship. And she wasn't minding that possibility the more she was with Dawson. "We could count sheep together."

Dawson laughed and opened his door. "Are you parked behind the building?"

"Yeah, but you don't need to walk me," she said.

He just opened his door the rest of the way and hopped out.

"Stubborn man," she said under her breath, but loudly enough for him to hear.

As he walked around the truck to open her door, Clara took off her seatbelt and picked up her purse.

They'd had a fun night together. There'd been plenty of

flirting, but some somber talk as well. Dawson's phone had stayed off the whole time, and Clara had fallen asleep against him. She was starting to seriously wonder why his ex-wife had treated him so poorly. Yeah, it was obvious Dawson wasn't perfect and perhaps worked way too much, but he was willing to listen, quick to apologize, and definitely aware that he had faults.

It was all sort of endearing.

Dawson opened her door, and she placed her hand in his as she climbed out. They walked hand in hand through the alleyway leading to the back of the building where a parking lot led to another exit.

Dawson didn't speak as they walked, and neither did Clara, even though a dozen thoughts seemed to be going through her head. Things seemed more intimate between them, and she couldn't figure out exactly what had changed. Maybe it was hearing that Dawson's ex-wife had blindsided him just as Max had blindsided Clara.

When they reached her car, she turned and looked up at him. He simply gazed back as she scanned his face, the slightly messy look of his hair, and the wrinkles on his dress shirt, likely from her. He'd taken his tie and suit coat off before they'd gone into the restaurant, and Clara sort of loved how he dressed up most of the time. Although, she equally liked him in a T-shirt. The top buttons of his dress shirt were undone, and she wanted to lean in and press a kiss against the beating pulse at the base of his throat.

The desire startled her and should have forced her to release his hand, to step away, and to collect her thoughts.

Instead, she said, "So, I was thinking, if you're not busy Friday night I'd cook you dinner."

Dawson blinked. Then a slow smile grew on his face. "Are you being serious?"

"Yes, are you busy Friday night?"

"I can be persuaded to keep it open for you."

She smiled back and released his hand. "Great. My place or yours?"

He paused. "My place. I don't want you to think I'm hiding anything from you. In fact, you can search my condo for any dark secrets."

Clara laughed. "I'll keep that in mind." She reached into her purse and pulled out her keys. "Thanks for dinner, and everything. I had fun tonight."

He nodded, shoving his hands into his pockets. "Me too, Clara."

The way he said her name was so tender that her heart hitched. She could tell he was using a great deal of self-control, keeping his hands in his pockets and not teasing her about kissing anymore.

She opened her door and climbed in, then started her car. Of course, Dawson remained standing there as she pulled away and headed for the parking lot exit. She slowed before turning onto the street and checked her rearview mirror. Dawson was still standing there, hands in his pockets, watching after her.

A lump formed in her throat, and she was confounded by the emotion that surged through her. Before she could talk herself out of her next impulse, she put her car into park and opened her door. Leaving the car door open, she hurried back across the parking lot to where Dawson was standing.

His brows rose. "Did you forget something?"

"Yes," she said in a breathless voice. When she reached him, she grasped the front of his shirt and tugged him toward her.

He didn't resist, and she slid her arms around his neck and pressed her mouth against his.

She was pretty sure she'd imagined kissing Dawson a time or two, but the fantasy was not as good as the reality.

Dawson rested his hands on her hips and drew her flush against him as he kissed her back. His mouth was warm, his lips searching, and his heart was thudding nearly as hard as hers. Everything inside her heated as their kissing turned exploratory, and Dawson slid his hands behind her back and lifted her up.

She tightened her hold around his shoulders and squealed as he slowly spun her around. He didn't stop kissing her though, and eventually he set her down. He ran his hands up her back, over her shoulders, then cradled her face. "Clara," he whispered, but then didn't give her a chance to answer.

His mouth was distracting her from all cognitive thought, and she knew she'd never felt like this kissing another man. Dawson was all-encompassing, and the taste of him and scent of him and his warm and solid body overwhelmed every one of her senses. When he drew away, it was only to trail kisses along her neck.

His lips against her neck sent a new barrage of warm shivers all the way to her toes. She moved her hand to thread her fingers through his hair and drew him even closer. Then he buried his face against her skin and pulled her into a tight hug.

Clara knew she could stay wrapped in Dawson's arms indefinitely, which probably meant she should release him as soon as possible and figure out the numerous lines she'd just crossed.

"Dawson," she whispered.

"Hmm?" He didn't move.

"I should go." She didn't move either.

Finally, Clara sighed and ran her hands over his shoulders and down his arms. She drew away. He let her go, but his intense gaze made her remember his every touch and every kiss.

"Good night," she said, taking a deliberate step back. She had to keep moving, force herself to walk to her car.

The slightest smile touched his face. "Good night, Clara."

She bit her lip, then nodded. *Now. Leave now.* So she took another step, then turned and hurried back to her car that was still idling with the door wide open. This time, when she climbed in, she didn't let herself look back.

Clara drove back to her apartment along the quiet, dark streets of Pine Valley. She couldn't believe she'd jumped out of her car and run back to kiss Dawson. Her entire body felt numb and tingly at the same time, and she wanted to laugh at herself, then groan in dismay. She'd just had the best kiss of her life, and it had been with Dawson Harris.

They were supposed to be friends, and even though they'd flirted with each other, Clara had had no serious intentions of kissing him and changing everything. Apparently, her subconscious mind had other ideas and had taken over her body.

Clara parked in front of her apartment, went inside, and, without even turning on any lights, went to her bedroom. She kicked off her sandals and climbed into bed, fully clothed, and pulled one of her pillows to her chest. She closed her eyes and relived every moment of her spontaneous actions and the way Dawson responded.

She knew, *knew* he cared about her. The way he'd kissed her and the way he'd said her name had been more romantic and sweet than any moments she'd shared with Max. Hadn't she been in love with Max? He had been comfortable, he had been her friend, and they'd kissed plenty of times. But none of their kisses had advanced to anything more intimate, and Clara had thought he was just waiting until they were married.

Now she knew better.

Kissing Dawson had made a few things very clear to her. He wasn't holding back any of his own emotions, and he was already invested. And that worried her more than anything, because with Dawson, his kissing her hadn't been flirtatious. It had come from his heart. And it had come from hers.

Clara buried her face in her pillow. What was happening to her?

Fourteen

"Your mother says you're dating someone," Dawson's dad said over the phone.

Dawson paused. It was about 8:00 p.m., and he was on his way home from the office after another long day. After the kiss the night before with Clara, he'd definitely consider them dating. But confirming that to his parents would be an entirely different story. And he didn't know if the newness of what was developing between him and Clara would be up to the task of his parents' scrutiny.

"Her name is Clara Benson," Dawson said. "And like I told Mom, we're friends."

"Uh huh," his dad said. "So you have plans with this friend on Saturday night?"

"I might," Dawson said, knowing that his dad would get to the point eventually. His dad was the kind of guy who could spot an accounting error with a single glance, and predict the next big stock market success. But when it came to managing family dynamics, that was Mom's field of expertise.

Dawson found it laughable that his mom had put his dad up to the task of getting him to commit to coming to a barbeque at his parents' home—surely Paula Smith would be there. Instinct told him it wouldn't do to offer to bring Clara with him. No, his mom wanted him at the barbeque, available and single.

"If you're available, we'd love to see you there," his dad continued. "It might be better if you don't bring your lady friend."

And . . . there it was.

"Tell you what," Dawson said. "I'm going to invite Clara, and if she can come, I'll bring her. If she can't, I'll come alone."

The other line went silent. Dawson could just imagine that his dad was trying to figure out how to impart this news to Mom. Dawson really didn't want to air out Paula Smith's dirty laundry, but it might be the only way to get his mom off his back about her. This was all getting ridiculous. His divorce had been traumatic enough, and now he felt like he was a twenty-year-old bachelor with his parents trying to set him up with a "nice girl."

"Thanks for the call, Dad," Dawson continued. "I just got home, and I'm beat."

"All right," his dad said. "Take care, and see you Saturday."

His tone sounded a bit distant, and Dawson could only imagine the report his dad would give to Mom.

Dawson climbed out of his truck and went into his condo. After flipping on the lights and setting his computer bag on the kitchen table, he opened the refrigerator. Not much selection. Grocery shopping might actually help, but even when he did shop, half the food went to waste. It looked like he'd be eating another freezer meal. He should have stopped to grab takeout on the way. But tomorrow, Clara would be cooking for him. She refused to tell him what she'd fix, but that thought would keep him content to eat something manufactured tonight.

He pulled out a box of some sort of chicken and pasta and set it in the microwave. While it cooked, he went into his bedroom and changed into some gym shorts and a T-shirt. He was tempted to lie down in bed and go to sleep right now, but his growling stomach would wake him in a few hours. Besides, he had an early morning court appearance he needed to double-check some things on.

So he walked back into the kitchen and grabbed a glass, then filled it with ice water. He leaned against the kitchen counter, waiting for the microwave to finish. He sent Clara a text: *Heating up a microwave dinner, wishing you were here cooking for me.*

He smiled when she texted back seconds later. *Chauvinist.*

So he wrote: *Amended to: wishing you were here.*

She sent back a smiling emoji.

They'd texted back and forth a few times today, but he hadn't brought up the unexpected kiss. He didn't want her telling him it was a mistake, and the fact that she was texting him was encouraging. It also made it hard not to just drive to her work or find her apartment and knock on the door. He couldn't ever remember being this anxious to see someone, especially when he'd just seen her less than twenty-four hours ago.

The microwave dinged, and he rose to open the door and pulled out the bubbling dish. While he let it cool, he texted, *I can bring over ice cream if you haven't had your dessert yet.*

She wrote: *Nice try. I'm still recovering from that seafood dinner. See you tomorrow.*

Dawson sighed. *Fine. Did we decide on a time? Or a menu? Do you want me to get some groceries?*

A few minutes passed, then: *I'll get the food, and I'll see you around 6:00. What's your address?*

Dawson sent over his address.

She replied: *Thx. Be hungry.*

He thought about sending something flirtatious, but he'd much rather call her or see her in person. His phone rang, sending a jolt through him. "Hi, Mom."

"Dad told me you're bringing that Clara woman to the barbeque." Her tone was brisk.

"I don't know yet," he said. "I'm going to invite her, but if she can't come, I'll come alone." Dawson knew his mom already knew all of this.

His mom exhaled. "If you haven't invited Clara yet, then why don't you just come alone? It would be fun to catch up on old times with Paula and her family. They're really looking forward to seeing you again."

"I understand, I really do," Dawson said. "Paula has a great family, and it will be nice to see them. But I hope you haven't given Paula or her parents any ideas about me being interested in reconnecting with Paula. Our relationship is in the very distant past, and when we broke up, it was for good."

"She's been through a lot of hard times, Dawson," his mom said, as if she hadn't heard a word he said. "I think it will be great for both of you to get to know each other again. You have a divorce in common, and you're both more mature and seasoned now."

Dawson gripped the edge of the counter, letting it take the brunt of his frustration. "We didn't break up because of immaturity."

"You guys had such fun together," his mom said. "Paula's mom and I were just reminiscing the other day about . . . "

Dawson tuned her out; he had to. He was so close to telling his mom that Paula had been with pretty much every guy in high school that would have her. He'd been naïve enough to think she really liked him, and that their relationship would be exclusive. She'd been the first woman he'd ever been intimate with, and so maybe that's why the betrayal had hurt so much. It might also be why he never confronted Romy about how late she came home at night. He didn't ever want to admit to himself that Romy was like Paula.

When it sounded like his mom was winding down a little, he said, "Okay, Mom, I should run. Long day, and I haven't eaten yet."

"You know you can stop over on your way home from work to eat," she said. "I can always warm up something for you."

Another frozen dinner, but different kitchen. Dawson didn't point that out. His mom ordered meals from a gourmet delivery service, so it was higher quality than the standard grocery fare. It was remarkable how hearing his mother's voice often made him feel like he was fifteen again.

When he hung up with her, he ate, then spent the next couple of hours going over the case details for the next morning. He hoped it would be a day of reckoning for his client, Mr. Peterson. The man had lost nearly everything in a house fire, only to find out that his insurance policy he'd been paying on for over forty years had expired three days before the fire. Dawson hoped to get Mr. Peterson not only the insurance money he was due, but a little extra.

By 11:00 p.m. Dawson was feeling completely exhausted, but confident about the court hearing in the morning. He'd researched every possible loophole and had a solid argument and evidence for each. He picked up his cell and wondered if it was too late to text Clara. Probably. Of course, she had said she had sleeping issues as well. But still . . . he felt like he had to walk a bit of a tightrope where she was concerned.

Her kissing him had made it clear that she did like him, as more than a friend, but he didn't want to . . . what had she accused him of? Being overwhelming. So he instead set his alarm for 5:30 a.m. so he could get a run in before he had to get ready in the morning. After setting his phone on the nightstand, he was surprised that a text buzzed in.

Maybe it was Clara, and his pulse drummed as he picked up the phone.

Hey Dawson, I hope it's not too late to text. Or if you're asleep, you have your phone turned off so that this doesn't wake you up. LOL.

Dawson scanned to the very end of the lengthy text and saw Paula's name. It was like someone had knocked the breath out of him. He scrolled back up to start reading again. Hopefully she was going to tell him she was annoyed with their moms too, and that she refused to be set up.

Your mom gave me your number and thought I should reach out to you since you're going through a hard time. I told your mom that I totally get what you're going through! My divorce was final about a year ago, and some things are still hard, you know. Like the loneliness. Not that I didn't make the right decision by kicking Greg out, but I'm sure you understand the mixed emotions. They're crazy! Anyway, you've got my number now. Let's talk sometime. Maybe grab a coffee or something. It would be fun to catch up. –Paulie

He'd called her Paulie, as had a bunch of kids in high school. With the reminder of the nickname, more memories came flooding back. He sat down on his bed with a sigh. One part of him wanted to ignore the text and delete it. The other part of him knew his mom knew Paula had his number, so if he ignored the text he'd hear about it. And waiting until morning to reply would only mean he would stress about it all night long.

So he typed a reply.

Welcome back to Pine Valley. Yeah, divorce sucks, although I'm now dating a great woman. So I guess there's life after divorce, huh? I've got a crazy work schedule, which I'm sure my mom informed you about, since she tells everyone. But I'll most likely see you at the barbeque Saturday. Have a good night.

He hit SEND and turned off his phone, hoping he'd been nice but obvious that he wasn't interested in "catching up."

Fifteen

Clara double-checked the address she'd plugged into her phone. Dawson lived only five miles away. All this time. She was surprised they hadn't run into each other sooner than that night at the yoga class. When she pulled into the condo parking lot, it didn't take her long to figure out which condo was his.

Before getting out of her car, she took several deep breaths. Kissing Dawson had been impulsive, and she was so grateful that he hadn't teased her about it afterward. He hadn't even brought it up or alluded to it, so she wasn't exactly sure what he thought. She knew he was looking forward to this meal, yet now she was a bit nervous to be in such a private place with him. What if he thought she was now infatuated with him, and he expected a lot more than she was willing to commit to?

Maybe they should have gone to a restaurant, where they'd be surrounded by people and music, and she wouldn't have to face the awkward conversation that was bound to happen when she told him that the kiss didn't mean what he thought it meant. She'd been impulsive, perhaps had even felt bad she'd teased him so much. But she knew they'd both been through a lot of pain, and they should be keeping things light between them. It was best for both parties.

Clara groaned, sick of her own philosophizing. Why couldn't she just enjoy making a meal for a handsome, charming guy without over-analyzing every single thing? Maybe they wouldn't even have to have "the talk", but she could make it clear in other non-verbal ways that she wasn't going to repeat the throwing-herself-at-him kissing episode.

With new determination, Clara opened her door and grabbed the grocery bags out of the back seat. She was going simple tonight—spaghetti, sauce, garlic bread, salad, and brownies for dessert. Easy and fast. If things were awkward, dinner could be made and eaten and over within about thirty minutes. She'd stayed in her work outfit—navy skirt and navy-and-white polka-dotted blouse. She was still wearing her wedge shoes, too, all the better to put her on more even ground with Dawson's height.

She made her way to the condo, set down two of the bags, and debated whether to knock or ring the doorbell. Finally, she decided to knock—less of an announcement. No one answered. Clara leaned closer to the door to see if she heard footsteps or any sort of movement. Then she turned to scan the parking lot. Yep. His red truck was there. She turned back to the door to knock again, when the door opened.

Dawson held his phone to his ear while he motioned for her to come in. His brown eyes connected with hers, and a jolt of heat went through her as she remembered the way he'd kissed her. She had to distract her mind so she wouldn't blush.

As she stepped across the threshold and passed him, she tried not to think of how his scent was now becoming familiar to her. Dawson answering the door while on his phone wasn't exactly the welcome she was expecting, but it took some of the pressure off. Dawson bent down and picked up the rest of the grocery sacks, then followed her into the kitchen. He was still wearing his shirt and tie. Maybe he had just arrived home himself.

Clara noticed that the place was clean—almost sterile, in fact. There weren't any pictures on the walls or decorations about. A half-dead houseplant languished on the coffee table in the adjoining living room. That room was stark too. The black leather couches contrasted with the white walls, and a flat screen was mounted on one wall, while the other walls remained bare. A bookcase in the corner had stacks of what looked like legal books on it. On the very top of the bookcase, she recognized the copies of the romance novels he'd bought. At least he wasn't trying to hide them.

While Dawson shut the front door and continued talking on the phone, Clara unloaded the food from the bags. It was clear he was talking to someone from his office. Some of the legal jargon went over her head, but she got the gist that it was a case between a homeowner and an insurance company.

When Dawson caught her eye, he gave an apologetic expression, but Clara waved him off. Busy was good. Busy meant they wouldn't have to have "the talk." They could take a few steps backward in their relationship and stay friends.

He perched on the edge of one of the kitchen stools, continuing his conversation. So Clara started searching through cupboards and located a pot big enough for boiling pasta, then found a smaller saucepan for warming up the sauce. She'd pre-made the sauce.

She filled the larger pot with water, set it on the gas stove, and switched on the burner. Then she poured the sauce into the smaller pot. Next she found a cookie sheet that looked like it had seen better days and arranged the French bread on it.

Dawson was concluding his call as she preheated the oven. She pushed buttons until it looked like the oven was on its way to warming up.

"Hey, sorry about that," Dawson said.

"It's okay," she said, turning around. He was standing right in front of her. Her heart about leaped out of her chest.

"Hi," he said in a low voice, his gaze steady on hers.

Clara swallowed. "Hi."

"You look nice."

If he didn't stop this, she'd start blushing. "Thanks. So do you."

One side of his mouth lifted while he continued to search her gaze. "Are we going to talk about the elephant in the room?" he asked.

Clara released a breath, then offered a nervous smile. "Do we have to?"

Dawson lifted a hand and smoothed a stray strand of her hair away from her face. The contact made Clara's face heat, when she already felt plenty warm from the preheating oven and boiling pan of water. Dawson's fingers lingered on the side of her face, and she wondered if he was going to kiss her, right here in his kitchen.

"We don't *have* to talk." His gaze dipped to her mouth.

Clara placed her hands on the counter behind her because she was feeling a bit unsteady.

He dropped his hand, then looked over at the groceries littering the counter. "Spaghetti?"

Clara was both relieved and disappointed when Dawson moved away.

"Yep," she said. "Does that sound okay?"

He flashed her a smile. "I'll try to save some for you."

The moment had ended. He grabbed the bag with the iceberg lettuce in it. "I'll wash this and start the salad."

Clara raised a brow. "I didn't know you made salad."

"YouTube can be very informative," he said, turning on the water in the kitchen sink.

As he rinsed off the lettuce, she opened the tub of butter she'd brought, then looked for a knife in the drawers.

He opened the drawer closest to him, and drew out a butter knife. "Need this?"

"Thanks." She took the knife from him. Her thoughts were whirring, and doing these simple domestic tasks in tandem with Dawson only made her want to tell him that she *had* meant to kiss him. And that she was starting to really like him too.

He was giving her space, that was clear. And that was the right thing, the *best* thing. But Clara was sort of missing him, even though they were in the same room together.

"What's in the sauce? Smells delicious," he said as he started tearing up the lettuce.

"It's just a tomato base with some spices and ground sausage bits."

Dawson paused. "You made it from scratch?"

"It was either that or Ragu." Clara shrugged. "Ragu's too sweet. I made the salad dressing, too, since I like to add a few extra things." Dawson was staring at her like she had two heads. "What?"

"You've been holding out on me."

"Believe me, spaghetti sauce is not hard to make, and salad dressing is even easier. You just have to make them in advance." Clara used a wooden spoon she'd brought to stir the sauce that was just starting to bubble. There was nothing worse than a cracked wooden spoon, and she didn't know what kind Dawson might have in his kitchen, so she'd brought her own. She turned the element to simmer so the sauce would be nice and hot when the pasta was finished.

Dawson was still staring at her, not moving.

She met his gaze. "Should I apologize for not telling you that I like to cook from scratch?"

"No, no." Dawson seemed to snap out of his trance. "That's the best secret you've ever kept from me." He dried his hands on a kitchen towel, then picked up the two tomatoes she'd brought. "Do these need to be washed?"

"They're fine." Clara studied him as he cut out the tomato stems. "You seem pretty handy yourself."

He shrugged and located a cutting board, then placed the tomatoes on top and started slicing them into wedges. "Like I said, YouTube is a great teacher. What other secrets are you keeping from me?"

"I wouldn't exactly consider anything in my life a secret," she said with a laugh. "I mean, I work at a real estate office during the day, read and cook a little during the evenings. Sometimes I go to yoga class. And sometimes I hang out with you."

Dawson grinned. "I like that last part the best."

If he wasn't watching her, she would have put her hand over her heart. He could certainly turn on the charm.

"So, no secrets here," she finished. The water was at a healthy boil in the large pot, and she crossed to the stove and dumped in the pasta.

"How was work today?" Dawson grabbed the cucumber, then located a peeler and started peeling it.

Clara felt like sitting down and watching this man in his

dress shirt and tie continue to chop vegetables. She knew it was a trip down a rabbit hole to compare Dawson to Max, but Max was more of an order-pizza-every-night guy rather than one who would do anything domestic in the kitchen—let alone work alongside her. The few times she'd cooked for him, he'd sat on the living room couch at her grandma's and watched whatever game happened to be on.

Dawson's way was much better.

"What are you smiling about?" he asked.

Clara looked up. "Oh . . . I was just thinking about . . . how you're going to get your nice clothes splattered with spaghetti sauce if you keep helping me."

Dawson tilted his head. "First, of course I'm going to help you. You're cooking, in my kitchen. And second, you're right, I should probably change." He looked back at the counter, though, and continued chopping the cucumber. Then he put the lettuce into a Tupperware bowl, along with the veggies. He picked up the sack of croutons. "Did you make these too?"

"No," Clara said, setting the French bread she had buttered onto the baking sheet, then slid it into the oven. "I'm not that crazy."

"Good. I was about to start calling you Julia Child."

She raised her brows. "You know who she is?"

"My mom dragged me to some movie that was based on her life," Dawson said.

"Oh yeah, the one with Meryl Streep?"

Dawson nodded. "I think it inspired me to cook more than it did my mom. Her main comment after the movie was that Julia Child didn't have to worry about kids running around while she invented recipes."

"You're an only kid, right?"

"Right," he said. "But if you hear it from my mom, I was like having a dozen kids."

"What? Bad grades? Always getting into trouble?"

"Good grades, and only got into mischief once in a while." Dawson winked. "My mom just has a low tolerance for anything that's not routine."

"Like me?"

Dawson rinsed off his hands in the kitchen sink, then dried them. He moved toward her and didn't stop until he leaned toward her and said in her ear, "You're the best part of my routine."

Her heart flipped, and before she could think of a reply or whether she should just get it over with and kiss him again, he'd moved away. "I'm going to change."

And then he was gone. Clara took the opportunity to breathe, and to think about what she'd gotten herself into. What did she expect, coming over here and cooking and spending even more time with Dawson? Especially putting herself in a situation where she was alone with him, making the temptation to kiss him all that stronger.

Being around him more, and thinking about kissing him again, was its own recipe that had an inevitable outcome. They'd be officially dating, and that would open Clara's heart to vulnerability. Something she wasn't ready for. Even though Dawson seemed to be a trustworthy guy, and she was seriously attracted to him, he still had baggage. And she had plenty of her own. Just what she'd heard about his mom worried her. If Dawson was overwhelming her senses, what would Dawson, plus his parents' expectations, do to her?

For some reason, she was missing her grandma even more today. Maybe a good, long talk with her could sort things out. But instead of letting herself get misty-eyed, Clara pulled out the brownie batter she'd pre-mixed. She dumped it into a disposable 9x9 pan she'd brought, pulled out the French bread, and put in the brownies to bake.

The pasta was nearly done, and she turned off the element just as Dawson returned. He was wearing a dark T-shirt and low-slung jeans. And he was barefoot. Clara didn't know why she found him being barefoot sexy, but she did. It wasn't something she'd ever noticed about Max. But things about Dawson were impossible not to notice.

"It smells great already," he said, meeting her gaze with a question in his own eyes.

"It's almost done," she said. "Do you have a colander?"

"Uh, no," Dawson said, walking into the kitchen and getting closer and closer to her. "That pot has a lid with holes in it though." He bent to search through some lower cupboards. "I just have to find it."

Clara averted her gaze, because she wasn't going to stand around checking him out. She stirred the sauce again. It was smelling good.

"Ah, here it is," Dawson said in a triumphant voice and held up the lid. "I can do it so you don't burn yourself."

Clara smirked. "Go ahead. Where are your plates?"

"In the cupboard on the other side of the refrigerator."

She grabbed two large dinner plates and two smaller plates for the salad or bread. She was impressed that he had both sizes. She had the table set in a few minutes, and with the pasta drained, she started to set the food out. When they were seated, Clara insisted that Dawson take the first bite. After dumping some parmesan cheese on his mound of spaghetti, he dug in.

He swallowed his first bite. "It's excellent. The best spaghetti I've ever had."

"Good," Clara said. "The leftovers are even better."

"So we have another date tomorrow?" he asked.

"Either way, you can keep the leftovers."

"Really?"

His boyish eagerness made her laugh. "Really."

"Oh, I almost forgot," he said, twirling another bunch of pasta onto his fork. "My parents are having a barbeque tomorrow. We can have the spaghetti for lunch, then go to the barbeque."

Clara didn't say anything for a moment. Meeting his parents felt so . . . official. "Maybe we can just hang out on Sunday."

"Oh, no," Dawson said. "Don't go dormant on me because my parents are involved. They won't bite, I promise."

Her gaze narrowed.

"At least, my dad doesn't," he said, then took a sip of water. "But . . . well, I don't think it's too presumptuous to invite you because we're practically dating, and you did kiss me."

Sixteen

Okay, so maybe it wasn't the best idea to remind Clara that she'd kissed him, because as soon as he brought it up, she looked away. Was she embarrassed? Or did she regret it? Clara didn't have a problem speaking her mind, so Dawson was baffled by the fact she didn't want to talk about it. At all, it seemed.

Keeping her gaze averted, she picked up her water glass.

Dawson had gone too far. "Just think about it. Maybe tomorrow if you think you want to go, let me know. I can pick you up, and we don't have to stay very long. Both of my parents know that we're . . . friends. So, either way, no big deal. I won't stare at the phone or anything, waiting for you to text. Well, I might a little, but not all day."

Her lips twitched. *Please smile,* he thought. *Please talk to me.* He liked the talking Clara much better than the quiet Clara.

She set down her fork and finally looked at him. The usual humor was gone from her eyes, replaced with worry.

"Are you all right?" he asked.

"I don't know how I am, to tell the truth," she said. "I want to go to the barbeque with you, even meet your parents, like a normal person might do. But I think I lost the ability to be normal after my grandma died. I mean, I keep telling you 'maybe' on things not because I'm trying to be difficult, but because I'm having a terrible time making decisions about anything."

Dawson nodded. He hadn't expected this serious turn in the conversation, but he didn't want to make her feel even more pressured. "Okay, how about I make the decision? We'll skip the barbeque. There will be other opportunities to meet my parents. Besides, my mom can be a little hyper-focused, and I don't want anything to scare you off."

She was at least watching him with interest.

"We can do something else, or like you said, we can do something on Sunday." He pointed to his half-finished plate. "Although I can't guarantee there will be any leftovers by Sunday."

Her expression seemed to clear. "I don't think there will be any leftovers at all."

"I'm saving room for the brownies I saw you bring in," he said. "With all these amazing smells in my condo, my neighbors are going to start pounding down my door."

Clara's mouth quirked. "Maybe Leslie is in a forgiving mood and will come over."

"Ha." He shook his head. "She hasn't even looked my way since I last talked to her. We were in the parking lot at the same time this morning, and I was fully prepared to say hi, but she ignored me."

She lifted her brows. "Maybe you should have taken off your shirt."

Dawson laughed. "If that's all it would take—not for Leslie, of course, but someone else I'm thinking of . . ." He lifted his brows.

She didn't laugh. Instead, she took another sip of her water, then said, "Truth?"

"Of course." Except, Dawson's heart was suddenly pounding. This could either be really good, or really bad.

"I like you, Dawson," she said in a slow voice.

It didn't ease the worry that was building inside of Dawson. Was this one of those you're-a-nice-guy speeches?

"When we first met, well, the second time we met, everything I said was true. And it's still true." She exhaled and looked down at the table. "But I've found that I'm liking you more and more, despite all of our differences."

Okay, so maybe this would be really good.

"I mean, I think one part of me wants to date you, but the other part of me isn't ready for a relationship." She lifted her gaze to meet his.

He wanted to lean across the table and kiss her, because this was exactly how he felt too, and he saw it as a small miracle that she felt the same way. It was at least something they could work with.

She lifted her shoulders. "I guess we are discussing the elephant in the room."

"Truth?"

She bit her lip and nodded, worry still in her eyes. He didn't like that worry there. "I like you, too," he said. "Although you've probably guessed that by now."

"You have been fairly persistent."

Dawson smiled at that. "But, like you, I've been through a lot of crap. So I can't agree with you more. I don't know if

I'm ready either, but I'm just following my instincts here—trying not to analyze everything too much, if you know what I mean."

She studied him with those deep blue eyes of hers, and in them he could see that she trusted him. That meant more to him than he could say.

"So . . ." she started.

"So . . . how about we take things slow, but stay open-minded," he suggested.

She nodded, slowly, and he could see that she was considering it. "No parents?"

"Definitely no parents," Dawson said. "I'll even block their numbers from my phone if you want."

Clara laughed. "You're a nut, you know that? If any woman wanted you to cut your parents out of your life, you should run far away. You're a product of your parents, and I think the result was a pretty great son."

She was making it really hard for him to stay in his seat and not grab her and kiss her.

Instead, he leaned back in his chair and smiled. "I'm glad, because even though my mom can be very persistent . . ."

At this Clara raised her brows.

"She talked me off the ledge more than once after I got Romy's list of failures," he said. "And my dad, well, he's just that steady type of guy who takes a back seat to every event, but he's always been there too."

"I'd like to see it," Clara said.

"What?"

"The letter—the list of failures."

Dawson opened his mouth to reply, but then shut it.

"You said you still had it," she said.

He nodded. It was filed with the divorce papers in the cabinet in his bedroom. He'd only read it twice, but that had been enough. His mom had read it, then told him she wanted to take it and destroy it. But Dawson wouldn't let her. He told his mom that it was a record of the only time his wife had told him her true feelings, and he felt like destroying the list would be invalidating Romy. Even though she'd divorced him, she had still been his wife. Apparently, he had some messed-up sense of loyalty toward her.

Clara was watching him expectantly as he processed through his thoughts. "Would it be so terrible to show me? Or are there too many dark secrets?"

"No secrets." He spread his hands. "You probably know most of my faults anyway. Knowing a few more won't hurt."

Clara gave him a half smile and rose from her chair. "I won't pressure you or anything." She pulled the brownies out of the oven. "Maybe I can read it while you eat brownies."

She was totally pressuring him.

He stood from his chair and started to clear the table. "I'll think about it."

She set the brownies on the counter to cool, then proceeded to package the leftover food and put it in his fridge. He stopped her from doing the dishes and took over the task himself. When he finished, Clara had wiped down the table and counters and packed up all the stuff she'd brought.

"I was thinking," he said, walking toward where she was leaning against the counter. She didn't move, just watched him approach. "I think if we're taking things slow and staying open-minded, we shouldn't have to rule out kissing either."

He stopped just a few inches in front of her and rested his hands on the counter on either side of her. They weren't exactly touching, but the way his blood was stirring, they might as well have been. She gazed up at him, unwavering, unflinching.

When she didn't say anything, he said, "What do you think?"

She bit her lip, and he wished she'd stop doing that. It only made him want to kiss her more.

When she spoke, it wasn't exactly what he wanted to hear. "I think I should see that list first so that I know what I'm getting myself into." She arched a brow in a challenge.

He leaned closer and whispered, "So what are you saying?"

"I'm saying," she said in a soft voice while she ran her hands up his chest and stopped at his shoulders, "that you should go get the list and let me read it." She smirked and gave his shoulders a little shove.

He straightened and sighed.

Clara folded her arms. "It might be good therapy, you know. To have another person's perspective who's not related to you."

She was probably right. Besides, they weren't so deep into their relationship that if she decided to bail now, it would hurt that much. Right? "I'll be back in a minute. I expect brownies when I get back."

She laughed. He didn't think any other woman could be more persistent than his mom. Well, now there was one in the kitchen.

It didn't take him long to locate the manila folder with his divorce papers. Paperclipped to the back was the letter. He separated the document, then walked back into the hallway.

Clara was sitting on the living room couch. Her shoes were on the floor, and her feet were tucked up under her. She'd put a plate of brownies with a couple of napkins on the coffee table.

He handed over the document to her, then sat down and grabbed a brownie.

"It's hand-written?" she said, turning the pages.

"I never thought it was unusual." He shrugged and took a bite of the brownie.

"I thought it would be more like a legal document—like a file of complaints."

"Nope," Dawson said.

Clara scoffed.

Dawson gave her a sharp look.

"Sorry, I'm not scoffing at you or at this letter," she said. "Well, maybe I am a little. Look at this first thing: *You don't separate whites from darks.* Is she talking about laundry?"

"Yeah," he said. "I did my own laundry, so I'm not sure why she was bothered about how I did my own stuff. I dry-cleaned all my work clothes, so it was just my jeans, gym clothes, and underwear that I washed together."

Clara was staring at him like he had a third eye. "Okay, I'm just hoping the other complaints are a little more serious. Laundry issues can be worked out."

He waved a hand. "Read on, therapist."

"*You don't make the bed.*" Clara looked up at him. "Sounds like you expected her to do all the housework?"

"No," he was quick to say. "I washed the bedding on the weekends because she'd leave me a note, but she was always asleep when I got up in the morning. And I did make the bed when she was staying in the guest room."

Clara frowned. "I'm not judging you, but this is kind of... off. I mean..." She looked down at the first page again. "*You never asked if I liked eggs.*"

Dawson leaned back on the couch and closed his eyes. "That's true. I didn't. And although I made breakfast food, I don't even remember if she ate the eggs or not." He cracked an eye open to see Clara smiling.

"What?" he asked.

"Why did she have to be asked? Why wouldn't she just tell you—*I hate eggs.*"

He shrugged. He'd asked himself that plenty since he first read the letter.

Clara flipped the page. "What did your mom tell you about this list?"

"She told me to burn it."

Clara raised a brow. "Despite my aversion to meeting your parents, I kind of like your mom."

Dawson set his arm across the back of the couch, right behind Clara. "Really?"

She smiled and looked back at the paper. "*You're cold.* What does that mean? You didn't want sex?"

"Just for the record, I never turned down sex with my wife," he said. "Romy was cold all of the time, and she thought I was cold too."

"Like your temperature?" Clara placed a hand on his cheek. "You feel warm to me." While she kept her gaze on his, she moved her fingers along his jaw, then down his neck.

When she rested her hand on his shoulder, Dawson felt like his heart might stop. "You should make sure my lips aren't cold."

She smirked, but then she did the most beautiful thing. She kissed him.

Dawson closed his eyes and kissed her back. He moved his arm down to pull her closer, and she didn't resist. Her mouth opened to his, and their kiss deepened. She was everything warm and sweet and intoxicating. Her hand moved to his chest, and she pushed slightly away from him. "I think I've verified your temperature."

He groaned and tried to pull her closer again, but she turned her head and started reading the letter again. So Dawson had to settle for pressing his mouth against her ear and inhaling her sweet citrus scent, mixed with the smell of brownies.

"*You don't like my friend Tammy,*" Clara read. "Who's Tammy?"

"Her best friend," Dawson said. "And it's true, I didn't like her. I suspect she was an alcoholic, because every time Romy came home from hanging out with her, she was drunk. I yelled at Tammy once for letting Romy drive home drunk and not calling me to come get her."

"I don't blame you, and I don't understand how Romy couldn't see why you didn't like her friend." Clara kept reading, then said, "*You lied to me about your schedule.*"

"I did," Dawson said with a sigh. "Whenever Romy wanted to double-date with Tammy and whoever her flavor-of-the-month was, I'd say I had work or something. When I tried to tell her that Tammy wasn't good for her, Romy would give me the silent treatment for days, sometimes weeks. So it was easier to just say I was busy."

Clara turned to look at him again. "I'm sorry you got blamed for something that wasn't your fault."

Seventeen

Clara hoped that she wasn't coming across as too sarcastic and disbelieving about the list of failures that Dawson apparently took seriously, even though he had a valid answer for each and every one of Romy's accusations. It was hard to keep reading the letter with Dawson's arm around her, and his random kisses against her neck. It seemed that checking to see if his lips were warm had opened Pandora's box. Not that Clara exactly minded, except that the more she was around him, the harder it was for her to keep from falling for him.

She'd hold the record for how many heartbreaks a single person could endure in a year. She couldn't say one way or another if she and Dawson really stood a chance at something long term. She had once fully trusted Max, and look what that had earned her.

She refocused on the letter. "*You wouldn't turn off your cell phone.*"

"It's true, but I can explain," Dawson said.

"Of course you can," she murmured, but she probably already knew the answer.

"It was before contacts could be put on emergency bypass, so I used to charge my phone in the kitchen." Dawson ran his fingers along her arm, further distracting her. "I had the texts on silent, but I figured if there was a real emergency, someone would call. My phone rang only a handful of times in the middle of the night in all the years we were married. I think only one of the times actually woke up Romy."

"What were the emergencies?" Clara asked.

"Two were drunk dials, and once my mom called because my dad passed out in the bathroom. Turns out he was dehydrated from the flu. A couple of them were from my paralegal—who apologized and said she'd planned to leave a message since she was calling so late."

"So, nothing like a secret girlfriend calling?" she said.

"No, never."

And Clara believed him. Whatever faults Dawson might have, or might be accused of, he wasn't a cheater. Since Clara had let herself be tricked by one, she supposed she was on alert for even the smallest of signs.

"Where is your phone, by the way?" Clara asked.

He chuckled. "In my bedroom."

"Did you make your bed?"

Dawson looked at the ceiling as if he were thinking hard. "I'm not sure, do you want to check?" He grinned at her.

"Funny." She flipped to the third and final page of the letter. There were much more serious accusations. "*Your mom doesn't like me. You only married me because I was pregnant. You didn't want another baby.*"

Dawson pulled away from her and leaned forward, resting his elbows on his knees. "My mom liked her fine. They weren't close, or anything, and Romy could be really sensitive to any of my mom's comments. Not that I blame Romy."

Despite the complexity of Romy's accusations, Clara's heart still went out to Dawson. She scooted to the edge of the couch and put her hand on his back. "What about the other things?"

"There's a lot of truth in them, but she could have turned down my marriage proposal," he said. "Not that it justifies anything on my part. She got pregnant, so we got married. I think the bigger question is what we never really talked about. Neither of us were in love with each other." He met Clara's gaze. "Don't get me wrong, I loved Romy in a lot of ways. I think we just both knew that if she hadn't gotten pregnant we might not have ended up getting married."

Clara exhaled, then asked the next question. "So how did the conversation go when she wanted another baby?"

"It didn't," he said. "After her miscarriage, in my mind, I thought she'd need recovery time—emotionally. Romy wasn't really herself after, so I told my mom about it because I was getting really worried. My mom told me about how women could go into post-partum depression, even after a miscarriage. So I started using condoms to give Romy some time to heal mentally and emotionally." He sighed. "It's my fault I didn't explain my reasoning. It was obviously a major issue that we avoided talking about."

She leaned her head against his shoulder. "What if Romy had brought it up, and told you she wanted another baby? Would you have said yes?"

"I honestly don't know," Dawson said. "That's sort of unfortunate, right? The answer *should* be yes, but even if I had agreed, I'm not sure that would have been telling the truth."

"I guess avoiding the truth can be painful later on," Clara said.

He rubbed the back of his neck. "I learned the hard way. But now, looking back, I get where Romy was coming from. And I get why she did what she did."

"But it's in the past," Clara said. "And you need to leave it there." She grasped his hand that was on his neck. "I agree with your mom. You need to burn this list and move on."

He moved their hands in front of them and linked their fingers. "I've moved on."

"You need to burn this letter."

He stared at her for a moment, then said, "I don't have matches."

"I do."

He raised his brows.

"In the emergency kit in my car," she clarified. "It's not like I planned this or anything."

He continued to stare at her, and she continued to stare back, not wavering her gaze.

"Okay," he said at last, then cradled her face with his hands and kissed her.

Clara let the kiss last for only a couple of seconds, and then she drew away. It was too easy to get lost in the warmth of him. "I'll get the matches."

Dawson didn't protest or try to stop her as she put on her shoes, then crossed the living room and opened the front door.

She returned a few minutes later to find that Dawson had brought the half-empty plate of brownies back to the counter, along with the letter.

"Ready?" she said. "Is there some place we can burn it without setting off a smoke detector?"

"There's a walking path that leads to a small park on the other side of the complex," Dawson said, his brown eyes focused on her. "No one will be there this time of night."

"Okay, grab your shoes," Clara said. She picked up the letter and folded it in half while she waited for him to get shoes. When he came back in the kitchen, she held out her hand to Dawson.

She felt relieved when he took it. She hoped he wouldn't change his mind. Whatever issues he'd had with his ex-wife, deep or shallow, he needed to move on from them. Which, of course, was ironic, because Clara knew she needed to move on from her relationship issues as well. Maybe burning the letter would be cathartic for both of them.

They left the condo, and Dawson kept his hand in hers as he led her between a row of condos and onto a walking path. He didn't say anything as they walked, and Clara wondered if she was being too pushy. Would Dawson actually go through with this, and if he did, would he regret it?

Once they reached a small park with a couple of benches and a jungle gym, Dawson dropped her hand and took both the matches and letter from her.

"Are you sure?" Clara said, putting a hand on his arm. "I don't want to pressure you."

Dawson met her gaze. "I'm sure. And you're right. Both you and my mom." He knelt on the walking path and tore the letter into several pieces. Then he struck a match and lit each section. Within seconds the letter pieces were curling into black masses, framed by small orange flames. As they turned to smoldering ash, Dawson stepped on them, grinding them down to nothing but black specs.

"You did it," Clara said in a soft voice.

Dawson pulled her into his arms. She wrapped her arms about his waist and rested her head against his chest.

"Thank you," he whispered into her hair.

She closed her eyes and breathed him in, reveling in the warm sturdiness of his torso. She didn't know how long they stayed in that position, but when Dawson pulled away, she felt like she was waking up from a dream.

"Do you want to watch a movie or something?" he asked.

Clara blinked up at him. "At the theater?"

"We could do that." He slid his hands to the top of her hips. "Or we could watch something at my house on Netflix."

Clara had a sudden flash of memory of spending nights on her grandma's couch while she watched whatever series Max was currently addicted to. She could barely follow the episodes because he skipped ahead on his own.

"Maybe," she said.

Dawson raised a hand and touched her cheek. "You choose the movie. I'm way behind in what's out there."

"You don't follow any Netflix series?" she asked, leaning slightly against his hand. Hanging out on Dawson's couch wasn't sounding like such a bad idea after all.

"No," he said. "I've watched an episode of a couple of things here and there, but the plot lines move so slowly that I get too impatient and give up. I guess I'm just a two-hour-movie type of guy."

"Huh."

"Do you follow any of the series?"

"Just one," she said. "I mean, I've started a few of them but haven't gotten through the full season with any of them."

"Which one do you follow?"

"*Jane the Virgin*," she said. "Total chick series."

His brows lifted. "*Jane the Virgin*?"

"It's funny, but a lot of women humor," Clara said. "Jane is the main character, and she's made a vow to stay chaste until marriage. Then at a doctor appointment, she's artificially inseminated by mistake, and she becomes pregnant."

Dawson was just staring at her.

She laughed. "Don't worry, I won't foist it upon you."

"No," he said, moving his hand to grasp hers. "Sounds kind of bizarre, but I'm willing to give it a shot."

"You really don't have to, Dawson," she said as they started walking along the path back toward the condos.

He bumped her shoulder with his arm. "I want to, so stop trying to talk me out of it."

Clara bit her lip, and Dawson pulled her to a halt.

"When you do that, it makes me want to kiss you," he said in a hoarse voice.

And he did just that.

Clara practically melted against him as he kissed her quite thoroughly.

"I'll keep that in mind," she said in a breathless voice when he pulled away.

They made it back to his condo without any more lip-biting or kissing. Clara took off her shoes and settled on Dawson's couch while he turned on the television with a remote that looked like it was straight from outer space.

"So, *Jane the Virgin*, huh?" he asked

"Like I said, we don't have to watch it."

Dawson pulled up the menu and selected the series. "Are we watching episode one, or are you going to catch me up?"

"Either way," she said. "I'm on episode thirteen, but there's a lot of complicated backstory."

"One it is." He clicked on the first episode and settled next to Clara. Right next to her. "Am I too close?"

"No," she said, smiling to herself and resting her head against his shoulder.

He moved his arm to accommodate her, and before she knew it, she was nestled against his side. She just hoped Dawson wouldn't hate the show and make fun of it like Max would have. Clara had learned quickly not to suggest her favorite shows to Max, because he'd ruin them with his snide comments. It was easier to watch what he liked, even if sometimes she'd rather just be alone.

Another red flag she'd ignored while they were dating.

Dawson laughed at several things as the episode progressed. This made Clara happy.

"I think this is the weirdest show I've ever seen," Dawson said as the credits rolled at the end of the first episode. "But it's funny."

Clara looked up at him. "I'm glad you like it. Now we have another thing in common."

His eyes seemed to darken as he gazed down at her. "Yep." Then he lifted his free hand and brushed his fingers along her jaw. "What I can't figure out is how that guy you used to date would ever choose another woman over you. And what possessed him to be serious with more than one woman at a time?"

Clara exhaled. She sort of just wanted Dawson to kiss her and not bring up Max. "Well, his other woman was the one he loved, and I was the money bag." She shrugged. "He wanted the best of both, I guess."

"Money bag?" Dawson asked. "Are kindergarten teachers making millions?"

"No," Clara said with a laugh. "My grandparents' property is prime real estate. They were offered a purchase price more than once by the city, but they always turned it down."

"But you sold it, right?" he said.

"I accepted the offer on the house and land," she said. "After I consulted with my boss, of course. It should close in a couple of weeks. I'll have to go back home to sign papers."

Dawson leaned over and kissed the top of her head. "I'll go with you."

For some reason, this made Clara's eyes burn. She

blinked and looked back toward the television. "We can watch something else if you want."

"Oh, no," Dawson said. "I definitely have to find out how Jane is going to tell her boyfriend she's pregnant."

Eighteen

Dawson slowly came awake, and he stretched, glad he'd finally gotten some deep sleep. Then his foot hit something hard, and he opened his eyes. How had he fallen asleep on his couch?

The events from the night before came back into focus. After a couple of Netflix episodes, he'd watched a movie with Clara—some romantic comedy she'd chosen.

He must have fallen asleep, and then she'd left.

Dawson groaned and sat up. Sure enough, her shoes and all the stuff she'd brought over were gone. He didn't like the fact that she'd had to show herself out while he was crashed out on the couch.

He rose and stretched, a bit achy. The microwave clock told him it was just after 8:00 a.m. He guessed he'd fallen asleep sometime after 11:00 p.m. Well, he had been tired, but he'd had no intention of becoming that negligent with Clara over. He hoped she wasn't mad at him.

Walking into his bedroom, he unplugged his phone from its charger and sat on the edge of his bed to see what he'd missed in the past fourteen hours. It was pretty much a record for him.

Two calls from his mom, along with three calls from his paralegal—all with attached messages. A handful of texts, and thirty-three emails. Not bad. Nothing had burned down, and no one had died.

Instead of returning any of the messages, or opening any emails, he leaned back on the pillows on the bed and called Clara.

She didn't answer, so he sent her a text. *Sorry for falling asleep on you. I hope you got home okay.*

After showering and digging into the emails on his laptop, and no reply from Clara, he called his mom back.

"Did you get my message?" she asked the moment she answered the phone.

"The one about the rain forecast?" he asked.

"Yes, but we're still having the barbeque," she said. "We'll just plan to eat indoors."

"All right, that sounds good." He wondered where Clara was and why she hadn't called.

His mom paused, and Dawson already knew what she was going to ask. "Is your friend coming tonight?"

"I'm not sure," he said. After last night, he thought maybe Clara would agree to come. They were practically a couple, considering all of the kissing they'd done last night, as well as the burning letter in the park.

Dawson had to admit he felt lighter, and somehow freer, with that letter destroyed. "I burned Romy's letter last night."

"I'm glad," his mom said. "I was hoping you'd get rid of it."

"Well, Clara had the same idea as you, and after I thought more about it, I agreed." He exhaled. "I think it was a good move and will help me move forward."

Despite his mom's focus on the barbeque, and having him spend time with Paula Smith, she knew burning the letter was a big deal. "It was a good move, and I'm glad Clara thought so too. If you need to bring her, then bring her."

Dawson almost laughed at the way his mom's tone said anything *but* bring Clara. He also wasn't going to admit that he'd communicated with Paula either, because then his mom would just ask more questions.

"I'll let you know one way or the other," Dawson told his mom. "I've got to catch up on a few things now." When he hung up, he checked his phone to make sure he hadn't missed any call or text from Clara. Maybe she'd gone to a yoga class and didn't have her phone on her.

So he returned to his laptop, and it wasn't until his stomach started grumbling that he realized another two hours had passed. He moved to the fridge and started to warm up the leftover spaghetti.

Texting Clara again, he wrote: *Want me to save you some leftover spaghetti? Warming it up now.*

No reply. Dawson went ahead and started eating. Clara had been right. It was even better the second day.

He was rinsing off his dishes when someone knocked on his door. He froze for a second, thinking it was Leslie, but she wasn't speaking to him. So he turned off the water and dried his hands. Then he went to the door and opened it.

"Clara." He opened the door wide. She wore a knit shirt and leggings, and stood there with her arms folded as if she wasn't sure if she should have come over. "Come in. I was wondering where you went."

She gave him a small smile as she entered, her arms still folded. Dawson shut the door and intended to scoop her up into a hug, but she wasn't looking at him.

"Hey, what's going on?" he asked.

"Um, I went hiking for awhile up by the ski resort so I could clear my head after last night."

"What do you mean?" he asked. "I thought we had a nice time."

Clara wiped at her face.

Dawson felt as if he'd been hollowed out. Everything in her voice and manner told him what was coming and that there was nothing he could do about it.

She raised her gaze to meet his, and now that he could see her up close, her eyes were red-rimmed.

"Are you okay?" He placed a hand on her shoulder. "Clara?"

"I—I really like you, Dawson, but I just need to figure out who I am." She sniffled. "I just—when I'm with you, I feel like I'm becoming lost . . . in you. And normally, that would be a good thing because you're a great guy. An amazing guy."

Dawson tried to breathe normally. Clara was dumping him.

"I like being friends with you," she said. "But when I'm with you, it's just too easy to get into the other stuff." She took a deep breath. "I don't know if it's possible to separate the two. In fact, I know it would be impossible. When I left last night, you were asleep, and I thought about all the stuff you've gone through. You deserve someone who isn't skittish like me. Someone who can jump in with two feet and not have doubts."

Dawson didn't move for a moment. Then he squeezed

her shoulder slightly and dropped his hand. "What are you afraid of?" he asked in quiet voice.

She blinked, then brushed at the tears on her cheeks. "Of trusting in something that has no guarantee. Once my grandparents' house sells, I'll have nothing left. Nothing of myself. So I need to figure out my life and what I want it to be. I hope you'll understand when I say I need to do this myself."

He wanted to argue with her and tell her she had everything despite her losses. She had her job. She could make great friends. *He* could be her friend. She could start teaching again. But he told her none of that, because he knew she'd made up her mind.

He could see it in the determined lift of her chin as she looked at him and said, "I'm really sorry, Dawson."

He didn't move as she turned from him, opened the door, and walked out.

The door shut behind her before he could reach the handle. He rested his hand on the doorknob. If he turned it and opened the door, he knew he'd go after her. But if he dropped his hand, he knew he was admitting defeat.

Romy hadn't given him a chance to fight. And neither had Clara.

He knew if he went after Clara, he'd see the rejection in her eyes. In some ways, this moment was more painful than the moment he'd received the divorce papers. The divorce was hard, but when Dawson thought through everything, he knew it was right.

Clara . . . Clara was confused and still grieving, and he didn't blame her for pushing him away. But pushing everyone and everything away was wrong. They didn't need to date; they didn't need to be intimate. Yet, he wondered if such a thing was possible. Could they be purely friends? Especially when there was such a strong attraction between them?

Dawson turned the doorknob and opened the door to see her car turning out of the parking lot onto the main road. He folded his arms and leaned against the doorframe long after her car disappeared from sight.

His phone started ringing inside the condo, dragging him from his daze. The ringing stopped; then a few minutes later, it started again. He straightened and went inside, shutting the door behind him.

The caller had been Mandy. He cleared his throat and called her back. Work. Work he could do. Relationships, not so much.

He spent the next several hours going back and forth on a couple of briefs with Mandy, as well as taking a few calls from clients. Jeff called at one point, and Dawson thought about sending the call to voice mail.

But he picked up, and he was glad he did.

"Hey, Dawson, sorry for the awkward call," Jeff said. "But do you happen to know where Clara is? She's usually in the office on Saturdays, but she hasn't answered any of my texts or emails."

"Oh, she said she went on a hike, but that was . . ." He glanced at the time on his phone.

"Never mind, she's calling in right now." Jeff hung up.

Dawson's instinct was to wait a few minutes, then call Clara himself to make sure she was okay. But she'd made it pretty clear she didn't even want to be friends. He gazed at his phone for a few minutes, wondering if he should text her. Or maybe call Jeff back and explain more of what was going on.

But if Clara had called Jeff, then Dawson knew he should leave it alone.

At that moment, his mom called. Of course.

Dawson answered, "Hi, Mom."

"Oh, good, I caught you," she said. "It looks like it's going to rain for sure, so just plan on inside."

Dawson rubbed his forehead. "Okay," he said in a calm voice he didn't feel.

"So whenever the two of you get here is fine, but we're planning on eating around six."

He took a breath. "It will be just me, and I'll be there before six." Since things with Clara seemed to be at an end, it didn't mean he needed to wallow at home and make his parents upset he wasn't at their barbeque.

"Oh." His mom sounded way too pleased. "All right. See you soon, dear."

Dawson hung up, realizing his mom hadn't even asked what had happened to Clara. So much for getting any sympathy.

When it was finally time to leave for the barbeque, the rain had created puddles throughout the parking lot, and Dawson had to sidestep a few of them to get to his truck without soaking his shoes. He climbed in and started the ignition, then drove out of the parking lot.

He'd been doing his best to get Clara off his mind, not just because she'd dumped him, but because he was genuinely worried about her. She didn't have any friends in Pine Valley, that he knew of. There was her boss, and she went to yoga class. And apparently she also hiked. And he knew she'd be facing going back home soon to sign the closing documents on her grandparents' house. She'd told him she had stuff in storage still, and he'd offered to haul anything she wanted back in his truck. She'd also admitted to him that she'd be getting a good deal of money from the sale of the house, and although he didn't know how much it was, he knew that she could be even more vulnerable if scam artists caught wind of it.

Maybe he could tell Jeff to tell her to get an estate lawyer. He knew a couple, and one of them he highly respected. She was a woman, too, so that might be more comfortable for Clara.

As he pulled up to his parents' home, there were already several cars lining the neighborhood street. The lights in the house were full blaze.

Dawson hopped out of his truck and made a dash to the door, earning dozens of drops of rain on his clothing. He opened the door and was immediately greeted with delicious smells. And his mother's voice. She was an animated hostess, and he caught sight of her blonde, cropped hair almost immediately.

"There you are," she said, turning to see him as if she sensed the moment he walked into the kitchen. As usual, she was dressed to impress, her makeup and hair perfect, and her red-and-white blouse matching her red slacks. Her brown eyes, that matched Dawson's, assessed him. Then her smile widened. Which meant she approved of his wardrobe choice of khakis and a checkered, button-down shirt.

"I was just telling Paula that you'd be here soon," his mom said.

And that's when Dawson saw Paula. She looked the same as in high school, yet different too. Her blonde, curly hair was long, and she still had those green eyes that used to captivate him and make him believe he was her one and only.

"Dawson," she said. "Oh my gosh. You're, like, a man, now." She crossed to him and pulled him into a hug.

Dawson hugged her back but released her quickly.

Paula giggled, still holding onto his arms and squeezing his biceps. "You're so grown up. I can't believe it."

Dawson felt himself flush. He hadn't been a little kid

when they were dating. She'd grown up too, but how would he turn that into a friendly conversation?

"Mo-om!" a blonde girl said, tugging at Paula's hand.

"Hang on, sweetie," Paula said, patting the young girl's head. "This is my friend Dawson. Can you say hi?"

Green eyes peered up at him, then narrowed. "That's a weird name."

"Thank you," Dawson said, trying to keep the edge out of his voice. "You can tell my parents that."

Paula giggled. "Oh my goodness. Kids say the most horrible things." She turned a sharp gaze to her daughter. "Go find your brother, then I'll let you have some chips."

The girl hurried away, calling out, "Jack!" in a loud voice.

"Well," Paula said, turning back to Dawson and smoothing her hair. A gesture that was all too familiar to him. "Can you believe I have two kids? Kind of crazy." Her gaze scanned him. "It's sooo good to see you."

"You too," Dawson said. "I should say hi to a few people, then we can catch up."

"Sure." Paula gave him a broad smile.

Should he tell her that she had a green speck of something between her teeth? No . . . He headed toward the patio doors, greeting a few people on his way outside. Sure enough, his dad was manning the grill beneath the patio's roof. The rain made everything chilly, but Dawson preferred outside to the chaos inside.

"Hey there," his dad said, looking up from the grill. His dad's brown hair had long since gone mostly gray, but in a distinguished way. "Mom said you were coming alone. Did you see Paula?"

"Yeah, I saw her," Dawson said. "Can I help?"

"Nearly finished," his dad said. "You're off the hook."

"Okay." Dawson folded his arms.

His dad adjusted some of the pieces of chicken on the grill.

"You know she cheated on me," Dawson said.

His dad looked up, his brows raised. "Clara?"

"No," Dawson said. "Paula. I know it was in high school, and you might think how can anyone really be serious in high school? But Paula was not the girlfriend I thought I had. I was loyal, and she wasn't."

His dad frowned. "I didn't realize that, but people change, you know."

"I know people can change," Dawson said. "But I just talked to Paula, and even though it's been years since I've seen her, all of those feelings of betrayal are suddenly back. I know that I can never consider dating Paula again. So I just want you to know why I'm leaving right now. You'll have to tell Mom, because if I go in and do it, it will ruin her party. She can call me later if she wants any details."

"Dawson," his dad said. "Stay for the barbeque. We can explain to your mom after, but we've got all this food, and perhaps you'll change your mind about Paula."

Dawson exhaled. Maybe if this barbeque had taken place before he'd met Clara, he would listen to his dad and stay. But even though Clara had dumped him, in the short time they'd been together, Dawson had learned there were much better women out there, better than Paula, and even better than Romy.

He'd rather hear the painful truth from someone like Clara, than be ignored by Romy, or lied to by Paula.

"I won't change my mind," Dawson said. "I'll see you soon." He went down the wet deck stairs and made his way through the backyard to the gate connecting to the front.

By the time he reached his truck, he was fairly wet. He

climbed in, but before he drove away he sent a long text to Clara. She might never respond, but he had a few things to say.

Nineteen

Clara stared at her phone. Dawson had texted her. She didn't want to open the text message, because when she did, he'd know that she'd seen it.

She closed her eyes and dropped her head onto her hands. All the lights were off in her apartment, and the rain was coming down hard outside. It was just as well. The rain matched her mood and her life perfectly.

She was completely miserable.

So much for finding herself.

She'd been sitting on the couch the last couple of hours, wrapped in a blanket, watching the rain. With a sigh, she opened the text and read Dawson's message.

First of all, I wasn't planning on texting you because I know you need space. But I just left my parents' barbeque before the food was even served because seeing Paula again made me remember things I'd hoped to never remember. So I think I understand some of what you're going through. And I'm really sorry you're struggling. I want you to know I'm here for you—as a friend. Anytime. Day or night. With anything you need, even if it's just my truck to move your stuff. I apologize for anything I might have said or done that made you feel anything other than you deserve. I hope you're okay.

Clara blinked back the tears. The thing with Dawson was that she knew he was sincere. He really did hope she was okay. She leaned back on her couch and adjusted the blanket over her. She wasn't cold, but the blanket gave her a small measure of comfort. She took a deep breath and typed back: *I'm okay. Thanks.*

Then she turned off her phone so she wouldn't be tempted to call him. But, strangely, she felt a lot better. Dawson's text hadn't made her feel more distressed; it had actually been a relief, because now she knew he didn't despise her.

He was a resilient guy, and she started thinking about what it must have been like walking into his mom's house and being confronted by his old high school girlfriend. Clara felt bad for him and sort of wished she could ask him more about what happened. From what little Clara knew of his mom, she wouldn't be happy with him ditching the barbeque.

Clara was sort of proud of him. He'd gone from burning his ex-wife's letter to leaving his mom's barbeque when he didn't want to be around his other ex.

Clara lay down on the couch, tucking one of the throw pillows beneath her cheek, and closed her eyes. She didn't know if Dawson would still be available when she had found her own healing, but she hoped he would be. And if not, she hoped he'd find a great woman and be happy. He deserved it.

The next thing Clara was aware of was waking up in the

early morning on Sunday, still on her couch. She didn't move for a moment, as she remembered the events of the previous day. Her misery had faded, and she didn't feel as much regret as she thought she might. In fact, she felt some hope.

She decided she'd call the spa at the Alpine Lodge and see if there were any openings. She'd treat herself and then finish reading *My Lady Jane*. Maybe if she happened to run into Dawson about town, she could at least tell him she'd read it.

By Monday morning, Clara was feeling even better. She'd been able to get a massage and a facial the day before, and both had been rejuvenating. Then, she'd spent a lazy afternoon and evening just reading.

She opened the office early and was already in the thick of returning emails when Jeff Finch came in.

"You're here early," Jeff said. He was dressed up more than usual, wearing a navy suit over a dress shirt and tie. In fact, he was wearing what Dawson might wear. "I would have grabbed you something."

"It's okay," she said as he set a paper sack on his desk that was labeled Main Street Café. "I've already eaten. The coffee's on if you want some."

"Great, thanks," Jeff said, still gazing at her.

Clara kept typing away, hoping Jeff would get to work. When she called him Saturday to apologize for being incognito that morning, he'd just told her to take the whole weekend off. Now she wondered if Dawson had said anything to Jeff.

"Everything okay?" Jeff asked.

"Yep," she said. "I went to the spa yesterday. It was amazing."

Jeff's brows shot up. "Good for you." He looked as if he wanted to say something else, but then his phone buzzed. He pulled the phone from his pocket and turned away, answering it. While he talked to whomever had called, Clara continued through the emails.

The front door opened, and a client walked in. Clara didn't recognize the man in the pale-green shirt and khakis, but she only knew most of Jeff's clients by phone conversation. He carried a large envelope and a clipboard.

As the man drew closer, she could see that his shirt had a label on it—like a uniform.

"Miss Benson?" the man asked.

Clara met his gaze with surprise. "Yes?"

"I have a delivery for you," he said, holding out an envelope. "And I need you to sign here."

The envelope had her name on it, but no address. "Are you with the post office?"

"No, a courier service."

"Which courier service?" Jeff asked. He was off his call now.

"Speedy Couriers, sir," the man said, looking over at Jeff. Then he held out the clipboard toward Clara. "If you can sign here so the sender knows you've received the envelope."

Clara hesitated, but there was no reason not to sign for the delivery, so she took the clipboard and signed her name. After the courier left, Jeff walked to the front of the office and looked out the windows.

"He's not driving a marked car or anything," he said, turning to face Clara. "Were you expecting something?"

"No." She turned the envelope over and opened it. Then she slid out what looked to be a stapled document of about four or five pages. Sure enough, the top page was addressed to Clara Benson.

She started to read the first paragraph, and felt as if her heart had frozen.

"What is it?" Jeff asked, coming to stand by her desk.

But she couldn't even explain. This letter had been sent by a lawyer who was acting in behalf of her *father*—a man she hadn't seen since she was six years old. A man who hadn't even been in contact with her, or his parents. And now, he was claiming that he stood to inherit his parents' property.

She turned to the next page with trembling fingers. The legal text was barely decipherable, especially through her tears.

"Clara?" Jeff had crouched so that he was eye level with her. "Are you okay?"

She shook her head, then pushed the document toward Jeff. "It's my . . . dad. I haven't heard from him in years. My grandparents raised me, you know. There has been no contact between my grandparents and my father. And now . . . this." She released a slow breath. She couldn't remember what she'd told Jeff about her background, and she knew she'd told Dawson a few more things, but she couldn't bring herself to explain everything right now.

Her father had found her. Her father had known about Grandma's death. And now he wanted the proceeds from the sale of the estate.

Jeff skimmed through the pages, then returned to the first page and read it more slowly. "Do you have a lawyer representing you?"

"No," she said in a shaky voice. "Of course not. I'm the named beneficiary in my grandparents' estate. My grandma told me. Everything seemed in the clear when I listed the estate and accepted the offer."

"Yeah, I remember I looked over the offer for you," Jeff said. "When's the closing date?"

"Ten days."

"Do you have a copy of the will?" he asked.

She shook her head. Her eyes burned, and she wiped at them, trying to stop the tears.

"Hey, we'll get it figured out," Jeff said. "If you're named in the will, then there's no problem." He tapped the pages. "I'll call Dawson and find out what—"

"No," Clara cut in. "I—we aren't exactly on speaking terms. It can't be Dawson."

"He's not an estate lawyer, if that's what you mean," Jeff said. "But he'd be able to refer us to one. That's all. You don't have to talk to him."

Clara dropped her head into her hands.

Jeff waited, not saying anything. Then, finally, he said, "I won't call Dawson if you don't want me to, but I trust him to give us a good referral."

"Just wait." Clara lifted her head. "I need to go through line by line, then see if I can get a copy of the will. I'm going to do some research online too."

Jeff nodded. "Okay. Do you want to take the day off?"

"Maybe the afternoon," Clara said.

"Whatever you need, just let me know." Jeff straightened. His phone buzzed, and when Clara waved him away, he answered it.

Clara focused on breathing for a while. Then she read through the entire document, line by line, as Jeff took various calls, poured her a cup of coffee, and even fed the stray cat.

By noon, Clara had finished all the work emails, made a few calls, typed up two offers for Jeff, and had gotten nowhere on her research on *what to do when your reject dad tries to steal your inheritance*. She'd looked up a couple of estate lawyers. She'd call them when she got home.

"I'm meeting the Lovells in a few minutes at a property," Jeff said. "You can leave whenever you need to."

Clara looked up from her computer. "Okay, thanks. I'm pretty much finished, so I'll lock up the office."

"Let me know how it goes," Jeff said, a sympathetic look in his blue eyes. "I'm happy to make phone calls."

"I'll let you know what I find." She offered as much of a smile as she could manage. "Thanks, Jeff."

"Sure thing." He moved to his desk and gathered up some paperwork, then headed out the back of the office.

Clara was finally alone, which probably wasn't a good thing, because the tightening in her chest returned, and she felt like she was going to hyperventilate. She knew if she stayed in the office much longer, she'd probably start crying again, and how would that sound when she answered the phones? So she powered down the computer and set the answering service on. Then she locked the front door and put up the sign: *Showing properties. Please call or text us.*

Clara flipped off the lights and went out the back door, locking it behind her. All of the rain the last two days had made the air cool, crisp, and clear. Now the sun had heated everything up, and Clara tugged off her sweater before she climbed into her car. She rolled down her window and drove back to her apartment, trying not to think of anything.

But the tears had started by the time she got home, and she hurried inside. She made herself a sandwich and took a couple of bites, but she wasn't hungry at all. So she started calling the estate lawyers. After her third conversation with a receptionist, explaining why she was calling, and being promised that she'd have a return call, Clara decided to go on a hike to clear her head. And to do something to keep herself from going stir-crazy.

Just as she got into her car, her phone rang, showing the area code of her hometown. It was the realtor who'd handled the sale of her property.

"Clara, this is Deb Stansbury. I've got a notice here that there's a lawsuit pending on the estate."

Clara exhaled. "I received a letter this morning from my dad and his lawyer," Clara said. "I knew nothing about this until now."

"We can't close if there's pending litigation," Deb continued.

Clara knew this, but hearing it made it all the more final. "Okay, what do you suggest I do?"

"Do you have a lawyer?" Deb asked.

"I'm working on that."

"Good," Deb continued. "Your lawyer can see if there's any validity to the claim, and then we'll go from there. I'm just obligated to tell you that I also have to notify the buyers. There's a possibility they'll back out."

"I understand." When Clara hung up with Deb, she wanted to throw her phone and yell at something. Mostly her dad. The man who'd decided that drugs were more important than his daughter and his parents. Was he sober now? Or was he still an addict looking for a way to finance his habits?

Her phone rang again, and Clara answered. A few minutes later, she had an appointment with an estate lawyer on Thursday. She didn't really want to wait that long to get things going, so if one of the other lawyers could meet with her earlier, she'd cancel this appointment.

Then Deb Stansbury called again. "Sorry to call again. I was actually going to call you today with another matter, and I forgot to tell you in the course of our conversation. The buyers on your property have a partnership with a commercial company. There's a good chance that once the property closes, the house will be torn down within a couple of months."

Clara knew she shouldn't be surprised, but it felt like a blow nonetheless.

"You still own it until the closing date, and I know you

got out all of your belongings and furniture, but if there's anything else you need, you should pack it up." Deb lowered her voice. "I wouldn't normally tell a client this, but you could even sell the appliances, or cupboards, or countertops. There are salvage companies that will buy used items to resell."

"Okay," Clara said. "Thanks for letting me know."

After hanging up the second time with Deb, Clara felt as if she'd been run over by a car. She had no desire to go on a hike. Who knew how many other phone calls she'd have to field? She just didn't know how much worse this day could get.

Twenty

It had been over a week since Dawson had heard from Clara. Dawson had told himself over and over she was fine. That he would be fine. That everything would be fine.

But he missed Clara. More than he'd thought possible. Waking up every morning was like a punch in the gut, because he realized again that he wouldn't be seeing her or hearing from her that day. He'd been tempted more than once to call Jeff and ask a casual question or two about how Clara was doing.

But Dawson didn't know which details Jeff might know, if anything.

So Dawson did nothing.

At least his parents had gotten the message about Paula, and his mom even apologized. This made Dawson feel both better and worse. He really did wish Paula all the best in her life and hoped she'd find a man who would be a great dad to her kids. But Dawson wouldn't be that man.

Dawson had resumed his erratic sleeping schedule, but he made a valiant effort every night about midnight to go to sleep, at least for a few hours. So it was just after midnight when he found himself staring at the dark ceiling of his bedroom, again, and going over what he might have done differently with Clara. A knock sounded on his front door, and for a moment, he decided he imagined it. Maybe it was getting windy outside. A rainstorm was supposed to be coming in.

Then another knock sounded. This one he paid attention to. Maybe something was on fire in the complex or there was some sort of other emergency. A drunk and disoriented Leslie? He scrambled out of bed and hurried to the front door.

He opened the door to find Clara on the doorstep. Her eyes were wide, her cheeks stained with tears. She wore pajama bottoms and a tank shirt that exposed a portion of her stomach, and she looked like she was freezing. In one hand, she clutched a large envelope.

"Clara?" he said.

"Can I come in?" she asked in a shaky voice.

"Of course." He moved aside to let her in.

He shut the door once she was inside, then turned to her. Before he could ask any questions, she wrapped her arms about his waist. He didn't know why she was here, but she was literally trembling. So he pulled her tightly against him and rested his chin on her head.

Dawson closed his eyes. She smelled like sweet citrus, even in her pajamas. Her skin had been cool to the touch when he'd first hugged her, but now it was warming up, and he was warming up too.

Finally, when it appeared she wasn't going to let him go

anytime soon, he drew away. It was killing him not to know what had her so upset. "What's wrong?" he asked in a quiet voice.

She lifted her face, and her blue eyes seemed as dark as the deepest part of the ocean. "I didn't know where else to turn." She wiped at the streaked tears on her face and stepped back. Then she held out the envelope she'd brought. "Can you read this?"

Dawson blinked and looked down at the envelope. At first glance, there was nothing unusual about it, and he wondered if she'd maybe received correspondence from her ex-boyfriend. He took the envelope and opened the top tab, then pulled out the stapled pages. After reading only a few lines, he looked at Clara.

She had her arms wrapped about her torso as she stood shivering.

"This is about your *dad*?" From what he knew, her dad hadn't been in her life, or her grandparents' lives, at all. "Claiming his inheritance?"

She nodded.

"I thought your dad had left a long time ago," he said.

"He did." She rubbed her arms. "But I guess he found out about my grandma's death and wants money."

Dawson set his jaw. "Come sit down, and I'll get you a blanket. Do you want coffee?"

"No, a blanket's fine." She followed him into the living room and settled on the couch. He put the document on the coffee table, then left to grab a blanket from his bedroom. He returned and draped it over Clara.

"Thanks," she said, her voice more steady now. "I wasn't thinking too clearly when I drove over here."

Dawson settled next to her. "Not a problem."

"And I'm sorry it's so late," she continued. "I should have

called you first, but I would have lost my nerve. Did I wake you up?"

He shook his head. Then he met her gaze. "I told you *anytime*, remember?"

She bit her lip. "I remember. But you probably didn't really mean midnight."

He nudged her shoulder with his own. "I especially meant midnight."

A ghost of a smile crossed her face, and he wished he could pull her into his arms again. But he had to let her call the shots. So he turned back to the coffee table and picked up the documents she'd brought. He read through every line, and when he finished, he set them back on the table.

"When did you receive this?" he asked.

And the whole story came out. Apparently, a courier service had delivered the document to her office last week. After she told him about an appointment she'd gone to with an estate lawyer, and how the lawyer hadn't even pulled the will from her grandparents' estate yet, he said, "Okay, I have a friend I know from law school who works in your home city. She's an estate lawyer, and she'll get to the bottom of this in a couple of days."

Clara narrowed her eyes. "How's that possible? The lawyer I'm working with said this can take a couple of months."

"Yeah, that's a standard response. But sometimes it's who you know, and who you're connected with. Hang on, I need to grab my laptop and phone."

He returned moments later to the couch.

Clara had pulled her feet up on the couch and had the blanket completely covering her. The circles beneath her eyes were noticeable.

"Do you want to go lie down on my bed and sleep?" he

asked. "I can stay out here once I get a few things done."

Clara yawned, covering her mouth. "No, I don't want to put you out."

Dawson lifted a brow.

"Fine," she said. "But wake me up when you're tired, and I'll head home."

"All right," he said, knowing he'd just let her sleep. "First, though, for me to make any headway on this case, I need you to sign a representation document. I'm not an estate attorney, but I can get the process started."

"Sure," Clara said. "That would be great."

He printed the document from his laptop, sending it to the printer in the corner of the kitchen. When he retrieved the document, Clara signed it.

"Thank you," she said, her gaze meeting his.

He swallowed. "You're welcome. Now, go sleep."

She nodded, and he watched her walk out of the living room, her steps slow.

Then he called Lindsey Gerber. He didn't expect her to answer, but when she did, he wasn't entirely surprised.

After he explained the case and all he knew so far, Lindsey laughed.

"Wow, Dawson, I know you're a pit bull in the court room, but you're certainly going out of your way."

"Clara is important to me."

"Got it," Lindsey said. "I'll have something to you first thing in the morning. Send me the representation contract, and give me her contact information. Then I can copy you on the emails."

"Okay, great. Sending now."

After Dawson hung up with Lindsey, he went into his bedroom to check on Clara. She was sound asleep, and she looked a lot more peaceful. He pulled the blanket up higher so that it covered her shoulder, then bent down and pressed a light kiss on her cheek. Her breathing was deep and even, and he hoped she'd sleep through the night.

He snagged one of his pillows, then went back to the living room. It would take him a lot longer to fall asleep now, but that was okay. Helping Clara was more important than clocking in the sleeping hours.

When his phone rang at 7:30 a.m., Dawson sat up and snatched it from the coffee table. It was Lindsey.

He cleared his throat and answered. "Tell me you have good news," he said, his voice scratchy.

"Good morning to you, too," Lindsey said in a way-too-cheerful tone. "You owe my assistant lunch next time you're in town. In fact, you owe us both lunch. A scanned copy of the will should be in both yours and Clara's inboxes as we speak."

"Wow." He was impressed. "How'd you get it so fast?"

"I sent an email last night, and this morning my assistant waited outside the building until the first employee showed up," Lindsey said.

Dawson balanced his phone against his shoulder as he opened his laptop and opened the email from Lindsey. As he waited for the PDF scan to load, he said, "Did you look at it? Does her dad have a case?"

"Fortunately for your friend, the will is solid, and Clara is the sole heir," Lindsey said.

Dawson felt like he had a thousand pounds lifted from his shoulders. "Are you serious?"

"Yes," she said. "Her grandma was a smart woman. There's a clause in there that should anyone try to contest the will, they will receive a settlement of no more than twenty-five dollars."

"Twenty-five bucks?" Dawson echoed, leaning back on the couch. "Hallelujah!"

Lindsey laughed. "Agreed. I'll wrap up details with the mortgage company this morning. You owe us lunch and my fee of $650."

"Done."

"Have a nice day, Dawson," she said. "And tell Clara she's a lucky girl to have you in her corner."

Dawson swallowed at the compliment. "I will. And thanks for everything, Lindsey. I mean it."

He hung up with her and leaned his head back, closing his eyes. He was elated, and he also felt like he could sleep ten hours straight. Instead, he rose from the couch and went into the kitchen to turn on the coffee maker. He opened the refrigerator and was glad to see a carton half-filled with fresh eggs. As he cracked them into the frying pan, he wondered if Clara liked eggs.

She'd never told him when they were talking about Romy's letter.

The eggs were cooked and dished out onto two plates when Clara came into the kitchen. Her clothing was rumpled and her hair adorably messy.

"Hey," she said. "Smells good."

"Do you like eggs?"

She settled on the barstool at the counter. "I do, in fact."

Dawson smiled. "Good to know. Did you sleep okay?"

She nodded, then stifled a yawn. "Sorry about stealing your bed. Did you sleep?"

"I got a few hours in," he said, sliding over the plate of eggs toward her, then adding a fork. He didn't have fresh juice, so they had to settle for water.

Clara didn't comment, just started eating.

Dawson was more than happy to have her in his kitchen. He fetched the laptop from the living room. "I have something to show you," he said when he returned. He pulled up the scanned will.

Her eyes widened, and she set down her fork. "It's the will?"

"Yes." He scrolled to the third page, then pointed to a paragraph. "This is a clause that prevents anyone from contesting the will. Your grandmother put in a twenty-five-dollar limit."

Clara stared at it for a moment, then raised her gaze to meet Dawson's. "What does it mean?"

"It means that your dad is only entitled to twenty-five dollars," Dawson said. "I suggest we cut a cashier's check, mail it certified, and be done with it. Lindsey Gerber is going to contact the mortgage company so you won't have to deal with that end of things. She thinks you'll still be able to close on your original closing date."

Clara covered her mouth with her hand and laughed. Then she slid off the barstool and threw her arms around Dawson's neck. He chuckled as he hugged her back.

"You're amazing, Mr. Harris," Clara said. "Thank you, thank you! How can I thank you?"

She drew away, smiling up at him, and Dawson felt as if he'd already been thanked a thousand times over.

"We'll come up with something," he said.

"I know, I can cook dinner for like a month." She placed her hands on her hips and looked about his kitchen. "Or maybe three months." She sat back on her stool, then squealed, "I can't believe this!"

Dawson laughed. "I'd love you to cook me dinner, but you don't owe me anything. Really. I mean, unless you wanted to, but not to pay me back for anything. Your grandma is the one you should be thankful for. All I did was make a phone call."

Clara grabbed his hand before he moved to the other side of the kitchen island. "You've done a lot more, Dawson. You opened your door last night at midnight." She bit her lip. "You've been so generous, and I'm going to find a way to thank you."

Twenty-one

Ten Days Later

Clara stood on the sidewalk in front of her grandparents' house, her arms folded. The house was modest by any standard, but the surrounding acreage was worth millions. In a few hours, Clara would be signing closing documents on the estate, and she'd instantly become a wealthy woman.

She hadn't even told Dawson how much the property was selling for. Jeff Finch had reviewed the offer, so he knew, but she also trusted that he'd keep it confidential. And now that her dad's claim had been cleared up, Clara would be letting go of the property once and for all.

She had wondered if her dad would try to reach out to her after learning that he'd only get twenty-five dollars. She'd also wondered if her dad even cared to be reunited with his daughter after all this time. But so far, she hadn't heard from him. She'd grown up blessed to be a part of her grandparents' lives, and any grudge against her dad wasn't worth the energy.

Besides, she had a great man in her life.

The sound of Dawson's approaching truck caught her attention. He'd driven with her to her grandparents' home, and when she said she wanted to keep her grandparents' red mailbox, he'd left to get some tools at the hardware store.

She smiled as he pulled up to the curb, shut off the engine, and climbed out. No suit today. He wore what had become her favorite jeans of his and a gray, fitted T-shirt. Dawson had taken the entire day off to help her, and she found that more than endearing. She'd decided not to call a salvage company or sell any of the stuff off. She'd turn it over to the buyer, except for the mailbox. It had always been her job to get the mail, and the red mailbox would someday go in front of her own home.

Dawson walked toward her, a sack in hand.

"Looks like you bought more than a screwdriver," she said.

"I bought the basic tool kit," he said, holding up the sack. "I should probably have one stored in my truck anyway."

"To help more damsels in distress?" she said, looking up at him as he stopped in front of her.

One side of his mouth lifted as his brown eyes captured hers. "You're the least distressed damsel that I know."

She placed her hands on her hips. "Except when it comes to hiring lawyers."

"What's most important is that you got the right one in the end," he said with a wink.

While she watched him pull out the tool kit from the sack, then use the screwdriver to remove the red mail box from the post, she felt another rush of gratitude for Dawson.

They'd had dinner together every night since the day he

had called Lindsey Gerber. Mostly she cooked, but a couple of times they'd gone out to eat.

Dawson never tried to hold her hand. They hadn't kissed either. He was keeping true to his promise of just being a friend, no expectations. Well, they had hugged a time or two. Okay, three times to be exact. Clara pushed back the urge to wrap her arms around him now.

Each time she saw him, it took five or ten minutes for her heart rate to settle down, and for her to convince herself that friendship was enough with this man. Her pulse was increasing again, so she turned from Dawson and scanned the lawn leading up to her grandparents' home. There were plenty of weeds in the grass now, something her grandpa would have hated. And the bushes around the house needed a good trim.

It was sad to think that this could all be gone in a couple of months, replaced by a construction crew building a strip mall. Clara wasn't entirely sure what the property would become. Maybe one day, in a year or two, she'd come by again.

"Done," Dawson said, holding up the red mailbox. "Hey, there's something in it."

She turned to face him as he shook the mailbox. "What?" Clara opened the small door. Inside was a square envelope that looked like it was new, which meant it hadn't been sitting in the mailbox for long. On the front of the envelope, it read, *Clara Benson*, in what appeared suspiciously like Dawson's handwriting.

She looked at him, and he shrugged his shoulders, holding back a smile.

Clara opened the envelope and pulled out a card. The outside had daisies on it, but no words. She glanced up at Dawson again, but he kept his expression stoic.

Opening the card, she started to read.

Dear Clara,

I thought you'd like one more letter delivered to your red mailbox. I just wanted you to know how amazing you are. You inspire me every day.

Love, Dawson

She wouldn't cry. The card was sweet, but not a tear-jerker, right? She exhaled and met his gaze. "Thank you," she said, but it came out as a whisper.

"You're welcome." His words were simple, his smile sincere.

They stood there for a moment, looking at each other, Clara holding the card, and Dawson holding the mailbox.

"Do you want me to put this in the truck?" he asked.

"Yeah," Clara said, trying to come to her senses.

She waited while Dawson put the mailbox in the truck. He brought the tool kit with him as they walked up to the house. The realtor said her key would still work, yet it was a strange sensation to open the front door.

The musty smell hit her first as she stepped inside. Everything was dim due to the pulled blinds and curtains—curtains she remembered her grandma making. All the furniture had been removed, donated or put into storage.

Dawson came inside and stood next to her, not moving farther into the house than she had gone.

"It feels so empty," Clara said, turning to Dawson. "I mean, not just because all the furniture is gone, but because my grandma's no longer here."

He nodded. "You and your grandma are what made it a home. Without you, it's just a building."

"Exactly." She started to walk around the living room. There were markings on the walls from where her grandma had hung pictures. The carpet was still indented from the couch and coffee table. Dawson remained by the door, his free hand in his pocket as he watched her examine everything.

"The kitchen was my favorite place in this house," she said, moving to the adjacent room. "Come see it."

Dawson followed.

Even though the kitchen table and chairs were gone, the kitchen looked nearly how she remembered it. She'd always loved the small glass knobs on the cupboards. She turned to Dawson. "Would it be weird if I took off the knobs from the cupboards?"

He lifted a brow. "Do you have plans for them?"

"Well, when I get a place of my own, I'll put them on the cupboards."

"I like it," he said. "Do you want me to get started?" He held up the tool kit.

"If there's more than one screwdriver, I can help as well."

So they spent the next twenty minutes taking off all the knobs from the cupboards and drawers.

Once the knobs were in a pile on the counter, Clara led Dawson through the rest of the house. When she came to her grandma's bedroom, she stared at the empty space. "One summer we painted her room violet," Clara said. "I was about twelve, and I told her I wanted to paint her room for her birthday."

"How long did she keep it violet?" Dawson asked, coming into the room and looking around.

"About a year," Clara said with a laugh. "My grandma was a good sport, but I knew she didn't love it. So the next summer, we went for taupe."

Dawson turned to face her. "What color is your bedroom?"

"Come and see," Clara said, grabbing his hand.

Holding his hand felt natural, and she didn't let go. He didn't pull away either.

When they stepped into her room, Dawson chuckled. "Yellow. I should have known it wouldn't be a neutral color."

Clara turned to face him, their hands still linked. "Yellow can totally be neutral."

He lifted his brows. "I'm sure you have a good argument for it, so I'll concede early."

She smiled. "You're such a gentleman."

His eyes searched hers. "Always," he said in a soft voice.

And that's when she knew she couldn't keep him at arms' length anymore. She didn't know how he would react, but she wanted to find out. Still holding his hand, she lifted up on her toes and kissed him on the mouth.

He didn't move for a second. But then he rested his other hand on her waist and kissed her back. It was gentle, tentative, and not intense like the previous kisses they'd shared. He was letting her take the lead.

Then he broke off and gazed at her. "Are you sure, Clara?"

She nodded, biting her lip. "I'm sure."

He released her hand and pulled her fully into his arms, then lifted her up against him as his mouth sought hers again. She wrapped her arms about his neck and threaded her fingers into his hair, holding on as if she'd found an oasis. Which she had. Everything about this man was warm and solid. Safe. And she didn't want to let go.

When they both broke off to catch their breath, and Dawson set her down, she kept her arms around his neck. "I'm sorry, Dawson. I'm sorry for bouncing all over with my emotions."

"Don't ever apologize for telling me how you feel," he said. "Even if it hurts, I want to know." He smoothed the hair back from her face, then kissed her forehead, holding her close. "Do you want anything from this room?"

Clara drew away from him, linking their fingers again as she scanned the room she'd slept in most of her life. The yellow walls had been bright and cheery and had served her well. She'd had a happy childhood, and that was all she could ask for. "No. Unless I take the closet door."

Dawson chuckled and rubbed the back of her hand with his thumb. "I have room in the bed of my truck."

"Oh, I do want the mirror in the bathroom," she said. "It was my great-grandmother's—at least, that's what my grandma told me."

"Sounds good," he said.

They moved to the bathroom in the hallway. The house was small, and there was only one bathroom. Clara flipped on the light and stepped aside so Dawson could look at how it was mounted.

"I think it lifts right off a couple of brackets in the wall," he said.

"You're quite the handyman," Clara said in a teasing tone.

Dawson looked over his shoulder and flashed her a grin. "You shouldn't say stuff like that to me."

"What if I want to?"

He turned and leaned toward her. "Then I won't stop you."

She couldn't help herself. She kissed him again, then playfully pushed against his chest. "Get to work, handyman."

"Yes, ma'am."

She smirked as he grasped both sides of the mirror and lifted it off the brackets.

"This thing is a lot heavier than I expected," he said. "We should seatbelt it into the truck."

"I'll get the doors." She led the way down the hall and opened the front door of the house. Then they made their way to the truck, and she opened the rear passenger door.

Dawson set the mirror on the back seat and secured it with the seatbelt. Then they carried out the knobs.

Once that was done, Clara said, "Well, I think that's it."

He scanned her face. "Are you sure?"

"Yeah, I'll lock up, and then we can go get lunch before we go to the closing."

Dawson leaned against the truck, his hands in his pockets, as he waited for her to lock the door. She went back in the house one last time. This was it . . . the last time she'd see the inside of her home. There were so many memories she hoped she'd never forget. She smiled to herself, thinking of the new one she'd created kissing Dawson in these rooms.

She thought of how almost every time she'd left the house, her grandma had said, "Say you love me," and Clara had responded, "Love you, Grandma."

She brushed back the tears that had escaped, and took a couple of deep breaths. Then said, "Love you, Grandma," to the empty house. She closed her eyes and imagined her grandma responding.

Then Clara walked out of the house and locked the door for the last time. She took a deep breath and turned to see Dawson waiting for her. That sight steadied her, and she walked toward him.

She might be leaving her past, but she had a great future to move forward to.

Twenty-two

"Go," Jeff told Dawson over the phone. "Just get it over with."

Dawson scrubbed a hand through his hair. "I know, and I'm going." A few minutes later, he hung up with Jeff and gazed out his living room window. There wasn't much to see—a parking lot, then beyond that, the road he needed to be driving on right now.

He was picking up Clara and taking her to his parents' house for dinner. It would be the first time they'd all met. Ironic, really, that he was nervous now, because before they were dating, he'd invited her to meet them twice. First the symphony, then the barbeque.

Dawson exhaled. Everything had become more complicated lately, because he was in love with Clara. But he didn't know if he should tell her. It had only been a few weeks since she'd closed on her grandparents' house. And even though they'd spent almost every night having dinner together, mostly at his place, and she wasn't holding back in the affection department, he sometimes felt that things were still fragile. He didn't want to jeopardize anything.

She was trusting him, and that was important to him right now.

He grabbed his keys and cell phone from the kitchen counter. He'd made it a habit to turn off his phone Saturday afternoons and evenings—and he found that it wasn't as stressful to do as he'd thought. He could always catch up Sunday morning if he needed to.

Once in his truck, he made the short drive to Clara's apartment. They lived close now, but that might change soon. She'd been looking at one of the newer Pine Valley developments lately and had talked about building a house. This was good news, because it meant that she was looking at Pine Valley as a permanent thing.

He pulled up to her apartment complex, and before he could turn off the truck and get out, she came out of her door. Was he that late? He looked at the clock on the dash to see that he was fifteen minutes later than when he'd said he'd pick her up.

She waved as she approached and jumped into the passenger seat. "Cold feet?" she asked with a smile.

"No."

"I can tell when you're nervous, Dawson." She leaned across the seat and slid a hand behind his neck.

He leaned in for a kiss. "How?"

"You're late," she said, then kissed him. She drew away too fast. "You're the last person to procrastinate anything, but if you're nervous, then you're late."

"Okay, I'll admit it," he said. "I'm nervous about what you'll think of my mom."

"You're not worried about what she'll think of *me?*" Clara asked, her blue eyes widening as she teased him.

"I already know she'll love you," he said. "Once all the preliminaries are over."

Clara laughed and turned to clip on her seatbelt. "Then let's get to those preliminaries."

Dawson pulled out of the parking lot, then reached for Clara's hand. "Did I tell you that you're amazing?"

She squeezed his hand. "Once or twice."

When they pulled up to his parents' house, he saw his mom's silhouette in the living room window.

He jumped out of the truck and walked around to open Clara's door. He took her hand securely in his and walked her up the front walk. Then he turned the doorknob and knocked as he pushed it open.

"We're here," he called out.

His mom appeared almost instantly, followed by his dad. They were both all smiles, and Dawson let himself relax just a little.

"Welcome," his mom said, stepping forward and embracing Clara. "We've been looking forward to meeting you."

Dawson was surprised at the warm welcome, but his mom had always been a hugger, something that had annoyed Romy. She'd eventually trained his mom to stop hugging her when they met. Dawson was glad Clara didn't have such qualms.

Clara hugged his mom back, then shook his dad's hand.

"Thank you for the invitation," Clara said, moving back to Dawson's side, where they linked hands again. "Dawson told me not to bring anything, but I must say that I feel guilty coming empty-handed."

His mom's eyebrows shot up. "You're our guest, and I had everything around anyway. Besides, I wouldn't exactly say you're empty-handed." Her gaze went pointedly to their linked hands.

Dawson wanted to groan.

Clara only laughed. "Very true, Mrs. Harris. Dawson is quite the handful."

His mom laughed too.

Dawson stared. What was going on? His mom and Clara were cracking jokes about him within seconds of meeting each other?

"Come with me, Clara," his mom said, glancing at Dawson, then motioning for Clara to follow. "Dawson says you're a whiz in the kitchen, and I have something to ask you. We'll let the men catch up on whatever it is they need to catch up on."

Clara immediately released Dawson's hand, as if she were trying to get away from him.

The two women left the entryway and disappeared around the corner, with his mom asking Clara about the differences between some spices she wasn't familiar with.

"Well, son," his dad said, clearing his throat. "I guess it's just us until the dinner comes out of the oven."

Dawson met his dad's gaze.

"What's going on in there?" he asked.

His dad smiled. "Let's sit down and let the women get to know each other."

So Dawson sat on one of his mother's blue-and-white-striped couches in the front room while his dad talked about some accounting snafu at work. But Dawson could barely focus on the conversation and wondered how Clara was doing. Finally, he stood. "Sorry to cut you off, Dad, but I'm going to go see if Mom needs any help."

His dad rose to his feet too. "Sounds like a good idea to me."

When Dawson walked into the kitchen, he found his mom and Clara *not* cooking. Not even close. They were sitting at the counter next to each other, looking at a picture album.

Dawson came up behind them to see that this particular album was of his baby years. "Really, Mom?" he said. "My baby album?"

She ignored him. "He loved the park," she told Clara as she tapped a long nail against a picture of Dawson sitting on a teeter totter. "I used to have to drag him out of the park crying."

"Mom," Dawson said again, but to no effect.

The timer went off on the oven. Neither of the women moved. "I guess I'll get that." Dawson walked around the counter. He glanced back and caught Clara's smile. Okay, so maybe this would all be worth it in the end. He'd never imagined that his mom and girlfriend would team up together. He grabbed hot pads and opened the oven. It looked like his mom had made some sort of chicken casserole.

Since the table was already set in the dining room, he carried the casserole over to the dining table and set it down. "Anyone hungry?" he asked.

The women were still involved in their conversation, but his dad said, "I'm hungry."

"Great," Dawson said, narrowing his gaze and focusing on Clara, hoping she could feel it.

"We can finish looking at this after dinner," Clara said, rising. "Thanks for sharing it with me, Mrs. Harris."

"Oh, call me Nadine." His mom patted Clara's arm. "You sit by Dawson." She looked at him and winked.

Dawson was floored. He was thrilled, no question, but he almost wondered if this was some sort of trap. His parents had never taken to Romy like this.

Clara offered to dish up the casserole onto everyone's plates. She also said that she'd love to invite everyone over to Dawson's condo for dinner next week. "It's only fair that we find a way to thank you for your hospitality tonight."

"It's not hospitality," his mom said. "We're family."

Dawson looked from his mom to Clara. Was he in a science fiction Netflix series and he was just about to find out that his mom was a robot? It seemed his mom was now completely over the fact that Dawson would never date Paula Smith. He swallowed his first bite of the casserole. It wasn't half bad, but it was nothing like Clara's cooking.

The meal continued, and Dawson noticed Clara seemed to enjoy every bite of her meal. She even complimented his mom on it, which they both laughed about.

"No, really, it's good," Clara said.

His mom gave Clara a triumphant smile. Then his mom said, "Dawson tells us you like to read. Apparently you've been able to convince him to read a book or two instead of always being on his phone."

Clara's cheeks pinked, which Dawson worried about—was she embarrassed by his mom's comments?

"Well, we've read four of the same books so far," Clara said. "And I just might let Dawson choose the next one, as long as it's not a law book."

His mom smiled. "I agree, and I think that it's nice for Dawson to expand his horizons a little. Did he tell you about my book club?"

"He did, in fact," Clara said. "It sounds interesting, yet intimidating at the same time."

"Oh, it's great fun," his mom said. "You should come.

We'd love to have you. Although it's for women only. Sorry, Dawson."

"It doesn't bother me," he said, then winked at Clara.

From there, the conversation centered around his mom's book club, which his mom kept encouraging Clara to attend.

"I'll think about it," Clara said at last, after taking a sip of her lemonade. "Since Dawson and I are reading the same books, you could say I'm already in a two-person book club."

"Oh, what are you reading?" his mom asked.

And the conversation between his mom and Clara continued. Dawson and his dad didn't really stand a chance, unless they were occasionally asked for their opinions. But all Dawson was really required to do was offer a nod or give an "um-hum" once in a while.

Before he knew it, dinner was over, and his mom brought out a cheesecake that she drizzled with raspberry sauce.

"Wow, this is delicious," Clara said. "I must get the recipe."

His mom laughed, and Clara laughed with her. They already had inside jokes between them.

Clara asked his dad about his business, and he spent some time talking about the companies he managed accounting for. Clara looked duly impressed.

Dawson started to clear the table with his mom, and when they were both at the sink, she whispered, "You did well, son. She's a fine young lady." Then his mom turned away before Dawson could ask anything more. But he felt as if he were walking two feet off the ground.

By the time they got ready to leave, Dawson couldn't remember what he was worried about with Clara meeting his parents. He couldn't imagine the evening going any better than it had, despite the picture album.

"We'll see you soon," his mom told Clara.

"Yes, I'll have Dawson arrange a good time to have you over for dinner," she said. "It will be nice to cook for more than two people."

"Goodness," his mom said, her smile bright. "You are a wonder." She stepped forward and hugged Clara goodbye.

It was dark outside. Dawson turned to wave just before his mom shut the front door.

"Well, I think you impressed my parents," Dawson said, casting Clara a sideways glance.

She smiled. "Your mom is not scary, at all."

"I never said she was *scary*," he said.

"Maybe not that exact word, but you definitely implied it," Clara said.

They reached the truck, and Dawson opened the door for her. "I think she's met her match."

Clara looked up at him, arching a brow. "Is that a compliment?"

He grinned. "Of course. And it doesn't hurt that you invited my parents over for dinner. Romy never did that. I suggested it a handful of times, but she shut me down."

Clara nodded but didn't say anything. She climbed up into her seat.

Dawson walked around the truck and climbed in. After he started the engine, he said, "Do you want to come to my place? It's still early."

"You don't have a brief to review or a hundred emails to answer?" she teased.

"Probably, but they can wait." He grabbed her hand and linked their fingers, and Clara leaned her head against his shoulder.

"Then, okay, I'll come over."

"So, what did *you* think?" Dawson asked. "Besides *not scary*."

"They're great, Dawson," she said in a soft voice. "You're a lucky guy."

He was lucky in many ways, he knew. Just having Clara at his side, holding his hand, was enough. Seeing her at the kitchen counter, her head bent next to his mom's as they looked through the album together had done something unexplainable to his heart. And he knew he'd lost his heart to Clara completely.

He looked down at her in the dimness. She'd closed her eyes and wore a half smile. "Thanks for coming with me, and thanks for being your sweet self," he said.

She nodded but didn't say anything.

When they reached his condo, Clara said, "Next time they invite us, I'm bringing something."

Dawson chuckled as he parked the truck. "All right. I think the ice is broken now." He came around the truck to open her door, and they walked hand in hand to his condo.

Clara entered the condo first and turned on one of the living room lamps. She walked to the middle of the living room and stopped, wrapping her arms around her torso.

"Are you cold?" Dawson asked.

"No."

"Do you want a drink or anything?"

She shook her head.

He crossed to her and turned her to face him. "Are you all right?"

Her blue eyes blinked up at him, and he could see that there were tears in her eyes.

"What's wrong?" he asked.

"Nothing's wrong," she whispered. "It's just that your mom was so nice. I mean, she hugged me like she cared about me."

Dawson touched the edge of her chin and tilted her head up. "That's a good thing, isn't it?"

She nodded and wiped away a tear from her cheek. "It *is* a good thing. I just haven't had a maternal hug since my grandma, you know. And I never had a mom, and until tonight, I guess I didn't realize how much I missed out. I mean, my grandparents were great, so don't take it wrong."

Dawson leaned down and kissed her cheek. "I get it, and you can have all the hugs you want from my mom."

Clara released a half-laugh, then wrapped her arms about his waist and nestled against him. Dawson pulled her close, resting his chin on top of her head and breathing in her citrus scent.

Her body was warm and soft against his, and he knew he could be happy standing here, holding her, for a long, long time. "What do you think about joining her book club?" he asked after a moment.

"I think I'd like that," she said with a sniffle.

"Hey," he said, drawing away and gazing into her eyes. "Everything will be okay. Don't be sad."

"I don't think I'm sad, exactly," she said. "I think I'm so happy that I'm overwhelmed." She lifted a hand and ran her fingers along his jaw. "You're a good man, Dawson."

"Despite our differences?" he asked with a smile.

"Your differences make you amazing," she said.

"What about my flaws?"

"I can live with them."

"Ah, that's like music to my soul."

Clara laughed. "You can always make me laugh." Her hand slid behind his neck, and she pressed closer. "I'm a lucky woman."

Her hand on the back of his neck made him want to lean closer and kiss her. But he refrained, for a short time. "I'm the lucky one, Clara. And I should probably tell you, sooner than later..." He stopped talking, because he didn't want to be too impulsive.

"What should you probably tell me?" She held his gaze, her eyes a darker blue than normal in the dim light of the living room.

Dawson slowly released his breath. "I should tell you the truth."

She didn't seem surprised at this but only nodded. "Truth is always good."

"I don't want to freak you out, though."

"It's always better to know the truth, don't you think?" she said in a quiet voice.

"I agree," he said. "Even if it takes a pretty big leap of faith."

"Dawson," she said. "Stop stalling."

He almost smiled, but the truth was that there was a huge lump in his throat. What would she do? What would she say? "I love you, Clara. I have for some time."

She stared at him, but she didn't draw away or run out the door. Dawson hoped that was a good sign. Unless she was in shock.

"*Some time*?" she asked. "How long?"

This wasn't what he expected her to ask. "Probably longer than I realize. It might have started when you made me dinner for the first time."

One side of her mouth lifted. "Oh, really?"

"Or before that," he said, his gaze dipping to her mouth as he wondered if it would be okay if he skipped all this talk and just kissed her. "Like maybe when you first kissed me."

Clara smirked. "You're such a man."

"I'm taking that as a compliment."

She ran her hands over his shoulders and stopped at his

biceps. "You know," she said in a slow voice. "I think I might feel the same way?"

Dawson's heart felt like it might leap out of his chest. Literally. "You *think* you *might*?" He'd take *think* and *might* any day, but he wasn't going to let her get off so easily.

She pressed a kiss on his neck. Then another kiss on his collar bone.

"Are you telling me the truth?" he whispered.

"Always," she said, then kissed him at the base of his throat.

Dawson ran his hands up her back and into her hair. "Say you love me, then."

She drew away, but her hands stayed on his arms. "I should have never told you that about my grandma. Now you're going to use it against me."

"Not *against* you, but if it works to *encourage* you . . ." He raised his brows, waiting.

She looped her arms about his neck. "All right. You win. I love you, Mr. Harris." Then she kissed him, for real this time. No more teasing.

Dawson groaned and pulled her close, claiming her mouth, kissing her so she wouldn't ever doubt that he was willing to back up his words with actions.

"So," Clara said when they finally drew away to get in some breathing time, "when should we invite your parents over?"

"Really? That's what you're thinking about?" he asked.

"No, I was thinking about how you're an amazing kisser and how much I love you," she said, her smile growing. "That led to thinking about what you said about the spaghetti dinner, and that reminded me about inviting your parents over." She shrugged. "Truth."

"Okay, I can live with that," Dawson said. "Since it

included you thinking about how much you love me." He raised his brows in question.

"Which is . . . a lot?" she asked.

He grinned. "That's exactly what I was hoping to hear."

She laughed, and in a swift move he lifted her off the ground.

"Put me down," she squealed.

So he deposited her on the couch. "What are we watching tonight?" he asked, sitting next to her and handing her the remote from the coffee table.

She nestled against him and gave the remote back. "You choose tonight."

"That's a first," he mused.

Wrapping her arms about his torso, she said, "There will be a lot of firsts with us, Dawson. Get used to it."

He wrapped his arm about her while he turned on the flat screen. He fully planned on making sure she was right about all the firsts. And he looked forward to each one.

About Heather B. Moore

Heather B. Moore is a four-time *USA Today* bestselling author. She writes historical thrillers under the pen name H.B. Moore; her latest thrillers include *The Killing Curse* and *Poetic Justice*. Under the name Heather B. Moore, she writes romance and women's fiction. Her newest releases include the historical romance *Love is Come*. She's also one of the coauthors of the *USA Today* bestselling series: A Timeless Romance Anthology. Heather writes speculative fiction under the pen name Jane Redd; releases include the Solstice series and *Mistress Grim*. Heather is represented by Dystel, Goderich & Bourret.

For book updates, sign up for Heather's email list:
hbmoore.com/contact
Website: HBMoore.com
Facebook: Fans of H. B. Moore
Blog: MyWritersLair.blogspot.com
Instagram: @authorhbmoore
Twitter: @HeatherBMoore

MORE PINE VALLEY NOVELS:

www.ingramcontent.com/pod-product-compliance
Lightning Source LLC
LaVergne TN
LVHW021817060526
838201LV00058B/3415